I0602851

Cover Design and Interior Format

© **K**ILLION
GROUP INC

HEART
OF THE
GUNSLINGER

AN IMMORTAL WARRIORS NOVELLA

SARA
MACKENZIE

DEDICATION

To the fans who keep me writing

PROLOGUE

The between-worlds.
Domain of the Sorceress.

THE SORCERESS MADE HER WAY through the cathedral. Long red hair floated about her, her white fur-lined cloak ruffled by an invisible wind. Her slippers didn't quite touch the ground.

Above her soared ceilings so high they were lost in shadows, while candles set in sconces on the walls flickered and flared. The smell of incense filled the air, and barely a sound could be heard.

She came to the chapel she had been looking for, one of many that surrounded the ambulatory, and paused by the form of a sleeping mortal.

After her successes with Reynald de Mortimer, Nathaniel Raven, and the Black Maclean, she wondered whether she should carry on with her little hobby. For one thing, it was dangerous, and if her actions were discovered by her masters there would be repercussions. She could lose her position as ruler of the between-worlds and queen of time.

Another concern was that she might fail. She could never be sure whether the warrior she chose would live up to her expectations. If they didn't, she would have to admit defeat and send them on to Sigurd in the Dark World, or even to hell itself.

But when everything fell into place, when it *worked,* it was a heady experience. Addictive. Her powers were already great, but to reset a mortal's fate, to change his destiny. That was so much more.

So here she was, back again, and she had chosen her man.

Charlie Dawes.

His light brown hair reached his shoulders, and he had long sideburns shaved to a point. He was handsome, in a rough and ready sort of way, which was the sort of look that appealed most to the Sorceress. Yes, Charlie Dawes would do very well. It was time for him to become the hero he was meant to be. And she had chosen a worthy mortal female to be his partner in redemption.

Over a hundred years ago, Charlie had died under dubious circumstances and been forever labeled a 'no account,' as Charlie himself would say. A man who cared for no one but himself and barely warranted a couple of lines in a history book. The Sorceress knew his heart was in the right place; it was just his timing that had been off. Despite not intending it, his actions had ended up having dire consequences on others. Well, now he could put that right.

Candles wavered and the air hummed as if filled

with a swarm of bees as she began the chant. There was a crackle of blue electricity that grew stronger and brighter until it would blind any mortal who was present, and then everything fell still again. She could smell the faint sting of gunpowder in the air.

Charlie opened his eyes. They were as green as spring grass.

"Stand still, damn it," he muttered, still caught in the web of his past, and then he blinked and stared up at her. His mouth kinked at the corner in a cocky smile. "Well howdy, ma'am," he said. "Did I doze off for a moment?"

CHAPTER ONE

London, England

CHARLIE OPENED HIS EYES FOR the second time since he had died. There was a bright light above him, which caused a shaft of pain to pierce his skull. He blinked and tried again.

He raised his head and saw an oven. Shining metal benchtops were covered with bowls and other cooking paraphernalia. Something the size of a coffin, only upright and a bit wider on the sides, hummed against the wall.

Where the hell was he? It was a kitchen, but unlike any kitchen he'd ever seen before. A rack of trays holding baked goods made him think this was a shop rather than someone's home.

His back hurt, and he realised he was lying on the hard floor. He sat up with a groan, only to have his head start aching. He stayed still a moment, giving his body time to adjust. He tried to remember where he was, but there was a lot of fog in his brain—the unpleasant yellow fog that London was famous for, fog that stung your eyes and seeped into your nose and mouth.

The answer came to him slowly, a drip at a time.

The Sorceress had woken him up. He remembered her now, with her long red hair and vibrant blue eyes. She'd woken him up and told him he had to do... something. Charlie rubbed the back of his head, trying to remember what that was. He used the benchtop as a prop and hauled himself to his feet.

His warped reflection stared back at him from the shiny metal all around him. He wore a long brown jacket over his black button-up shirt with a golden star pinned over his chest, and he still had those goddamned sideburns that Buffalo Bill Cody made him grow for the show. Charlie was relieved to find he still had his favourite boots on under his denim pants.

Deadeye Dick. That was his show name and in the show he played a sheriff who kept law and order, and inevitably faced more than one shootout. But his real name was Charlie Dawes. A cowboy out of Arizona who'd joined up with Buffalo Bill's Wild West Show in 1884 and come to London a few years later for Queen Victoria's Jubilee Show at Cremorne Gardens.

And died. For a while, anyway.

He rubbed his head again and made his way to the water spout. At least that's what he thought it was. He fiddled with the dials on either side and managed to turn on the water, then ducked down so that it ran over his neck. The cold helped lift the fog. Suddenly he recalled what the Sorceress had said.

'Jennifer needs your help, Charlie. You failed last time. Show me you can do a better job this time. Redeem yourself.'

Who the hell was Jennifer? And why was it necessary for him to redeem himself? Failed? Failed at what? Sure, he'd been selfish, but he'd had a good time. Right up until he was murdered by the Duke of Bridlington, struck down like some varmint in the dark after an enjoyable afternoon in the duchess's boudoir. But that had been just bad luck. Could have happened to anyone, really.

The Sorceress had shaken her head at him. She seemed to be able to read his mind. And that was a mite worrying.

'If you pass my test, you will be free, Charlie. If you don't, you can spend eternity in the blazing sun of the Dark World, shooting at demons.'

That didn't sound too bad. It was more or less what he'd done in Arizona, although the demons had been coyotes.

'And every day you will die and spend the night in agony.'

That hadn't sounded so good.

"I'll do my best, ma'am," he'd drawled. Then he was here, on the floor, in this shiny kitchen.

Charlie noticed a plate of cakes with a cover over them and realised how hungry he was. He took one and bit into it. Another bite and it was gone. He took another cake, this one with a curl of fancy blue frosting on the top that spelt out a word: *Breathe.*

"What the hell...?" he muttered. Why would a cake need to tell anyone to do what came naturally? He looked at some of the other cakes, which also had words on them. There was *Breathe* and *Smell the roses, Laugh out loud, Kindness Matters*, and other equally odd phrases.

The duchess had fed him petite fours, if he recalled correctly, popping them into his mouth as she got him all worked up. But he got the gist from the Sorceress that he wasn't in the duchess's time any longer. He was in some other time now, and that worried him. What if there weren't Wild West Shows around anymore? What the hell was he going to do to make a living?

Charlie tried to remember the moment he'd died and found it to be a bit of a blur—the river close by and the safety of his bed just a step away and then the blade sliding under his ribs. He'd died almost instantly, so he supposed he was grateful for that. But the duke had done it to him, he knew that much.

The duke had been furiously jealous of Charlie's affair with the duchess. Charlie had started to get a bit concerned before he died. Wild Bill wouldn't want any trouble with the British government and the duke knew important people in that government. Charlie might end up getting thrown out of the Wild West Show. So he had tried to wean her off his services. He'd even introduced her to another man he'd thought might suit her, though she had insisted it was Charlie or no one, and the duchess was used to getting her way.

There had been plenty of other women besides the duchess, though. They were a bit of a blur now, truth be known, and it wasn't like he'd loved any of them. Or perhaps he hadn't *let* himself love them. He'd always kept a distance. It was safer that way, until it wasn't.

He knew why women loved him, though. He didn't mean to be vain, but he wasn't about to lie to himself, either. They enjoyed his looks and his place in the Wild West Show. He was exotic. He was dangerous. He was a notch on their belt, someone to boast about to their friends. Charlie didn't mind that. He had his own notches.

He'd made the most of his celebrity, but had no intention of settling down. There was too much to do and he was only twenty-five. It was better for both sides if he didn't let them think he was going to do anything more than love 'em and leave 'em.

There must have been plenty of mourners at his funeral, he thought with a smirk. Struck down in his prime like that. Something stirred in his mind then, something he knew he should remember, but in a flash it was gone again.

There was a window looking out to a patch of green grass about as big as a neck scarf, and he could see a grey sky. Was he still in London? He noticed the sticker on the side of the glass—'I ♥London' and a drawing of a clock tower that could only have been Big Ben. His question had been answered. There were times when he'd missed the blue Arizona sky and the blazing hot sun that hung over the red landscape. But most of the time he had thoroughly enjoyed living his life as Deadeye Dick.

He'd even met the queen. Victoria was an old girl, short and plump, but she'd had an air about her. He'd felt the privilege of being chosen to be introduced to her, and although he couldn't remember right now what she'd said—something about the weather being different—that moment had really meant something to a cowboy who didn't have a cent to his name, once upon a time.

Charlie had been famous. He'd performed in front of royalty and slept in the beds of the aristocracy, and for a time he reckoned everyone had wanted to be him.

Why, there was probably a statue in his honour out there somewhere, because that was the mark of a man who was truly famous—a statue. He smiled at the thought. Maybe he'd come across it someday.

There was a sound somewhere close by. Charlie stopped, listening carefully. He was no longer alone. Someone else was in the building.

CHAPTER TWO

BALANCING HER BAGS ON THE doorstep of the café, Jennifer turned her key in the lock. Nothing. It always stuck like this and she rested her hip against the door to give it a shove. It shifted. Another shove and she was inside. God, she needed to get that thing repaired. Her high heeled boots clipped across the polished wooden floor as she went to turn on the lights.

Winter in London had a reputation for murk and today was no exception. The lights flickered and came on. With a sigh she went to the counter and stowed her bags underneath. She cast her eyes around the small eating area with its retro linoleum-topped tables and metal chairs. Everything was clean and sparkling and ready to go.

It was cold, but heating cost money. Knowing she would soon warm up, Jennifer unwound her scarf and took off her coat, hanging both on the hooks near the door. She had some lemon drizzle cake to pull out of the freezer, but the rest of today's preparations had been taken care of the night before after she closed the café. Anything a customer might want warm could be warmed in the microwave.

King's Road was getting busy despite the early hour, with everyone hurrying to get to work. Occasionally one or two customers would drop by in search of a quick snack before they started their day, but Jennifer's 'rush hour' usually didn't start until ten. That was when the workers in the nearby businesses ducked out for their coffee and cake, before dashing back in again.

The Beatnik Café was in the right spot to become synonymous with the 1960s London music and fashion scene, although her grand-mother said there had been a coffee shop on this spot long before she'd bought the place. It had always seemed perfect to her, from the moment she first walked through the door.

Others must have felt the same, because it had become very successful. Gran often told the story of fashion designer Mary Quant coming in for her daily cup of milky tea; then there was the time John Lennon had sat down with a newspaper and demanded bangers and mash.

The Beatnik had its memories, and although her grandmother was gone and the cafe now belonged to her, Jennifer liked to keep those memories alive. The walls were covered with framed memora-bilia, copies of photographs, and signed napkins. The originals would have been worth something now, but Gran had sold anything worth anything before she'd died. These were all replicas.

Gran had tried to hang on to the café for Jennifer's sake and she'd made the mistake of trusting the wrong man. Jennifer couldn't entirely blame her because she had trusted Lawrie too. He had been a friend to Gran. And it pained Jennifer to admit it, but she had seen him as a father figure. There were times when she had confided in him, let him give her a friendly hug when Gran's illness got her down. By the time she knew better it was too late. And it turned out it wasn't just the café and her grandmother's legacy that Lawrie was after.

They'd had a conversation last week. Lawrie made himself comfortable until the café emptied and then pretended to sympathise with her about her situation.

"You know," he said, *"there is a way out of all of this, Jennifer. A way that would be mutually beneficial to us both."*

"And what way is that?"

His dark eyes slid over her and she felt dirty. She didn't even wait for him to say the words.

"Get out."

He shook his head. "I like you, Jennifer. I don't think you understand—"

"I understand, all right. Get out. Now." She marched to the door and held it open.

She felt a niggle of fear as he stared at her, wondering if he would obey her and what she would do if he didn't. Then he got up. The chair slid back and hit the wall. He moved toward her and she took a step back despite herself. He smiled, sensing her fear and enjoying it.

"I'm going." He leaned down from his greater height,

his face too close to hers. The lines on his face deepened and he looked every bit of his fifty-plus years. "But you know I'll be back, Jennifer. You know it."

Jennifer shook off the unpleasant memory. She had spent enough time worrying about his behaviour. Yes, Lawrie would have to be dealt with, but not right now.

She bent down to peer through the glass display of the counter. Everything looked good. Lemon tarts and almond cakes, chocolate brownies and affirmation cupcakes. There were some savoury snacks for those who didn't have a sweet tooth, although in Jennifer's experience that wasn't many.

Pleased with the display, she moved to the coffee machine and began to sort mugs, as well as cups and saucers for the confirmed tea drinkers. There was a selection of milk—cow, goat, soy, almond, and coconut—and sweeteners in an equally varied selection.

All set. Time to tell the world she was open.

She was about to flip over the sign hanging on the glass panel of the door when it was shoved open so violently that it almost knocked her over.

Two men forced their way inside. They were big and bulky, wearing jeans and jackets, with beanies pulled over their hair. The smell of their sweat stung her nostrils.

"You owe Lawrie money, bitch," one of them said, or that was what she thought he said. His accent was thick.

The door closed behind them and Jennifer

found herself up against the counter with one of the men right in her face. His skin was pitted and there was a sore on his lip, but it was his eyes that frightened her the most. They were like black holes without feeling.

"Why are you doing this? We had an agreement. I know I didn't make the payment this month, but things have been—" she began.

"No more excuses, bitch," the man growled. "He wants his money *now*."

Jennifer tried to stomp on the man's instep, but he was ready for her, and shoved her back, pinning her legs to the counter with his.

"Nuh-uh." He grinned, and the smell of his breath turned her stomach.

"Let me go," she cried out, embarrassed to hear the betraying tremor in her voice.

His hand closed around her arm and he squeezed. She tried to pull away, but he just laughed and shook her. "We're here to take you to him, understand?" he said. "He's sick of waiting."

She had rejected Lawrie and now he was forcing her to agree to his terms. Jennifer was no coward, but she wasn't a fool either. She needed help.

Before she could cry out, a new voice came from behind her, near the kitchen.

"My advice, fellas, is to let the little lady go and be on your way."

The two men looked up past her. The one who held her dropped his hand and she stumbled around the counter, bumping her hip on the rounded corner as she put it between her and the thugs. Only then did she feel safe enough to turn her attention to the man behind that drawling American voice.

Jennifer couldn't believe her eyes. A cowboy, just like in *Deadwood* or *High Noon*, one of her grandmother's favourite movies. Whoever he was, he wore a brown jacket and a black shirt with fancy stitching on it, teamed with jeans and tasselled boots. And he was holding a gun—a Colt Army Revolver. She knew a bit about guns from an old boyfriend.

The man's caramel hair brushed his shoulders, and his sideburns covered a chiselled, handsome face. And—and this was the most bizarre thing of all—he had a sheriff's gold star pinned on his chest.

Kiss me, sheriff.

She had to be suffering from some sort of brain trauma to even think that this was really happening. She half-expected to swoon and cry out "My hero," like some damsel being untied from the railroad tracks.

The gunslinger's eyes flicked towards her, green and full of questions. Then they slid back to the men on the other side of the counter, and his lip curled with scorn.

"Oh please," he drawled in disgust.

One of the men had taken a knife from behind his back and was holding it out threateningly. "Look at mister cosplay here. That thing's just a toy."

The gunslinger raised the pistol and pulled back

the hammer. The harsh metal on metal *cli-clack* certainly sounded real enough.

"Wanna bet?"

It turned out neither was the betting type. The two men turned and fled, banging the door so hard behind them the glass panel cracked.

Jennifer put a hand on her chest. Her heart was pounding wildly and she tried to gather her thoughts, and her breath. Apart from the damaged window, the shop looked okay, everything was in its place, and she could hear the traffic outside. The world was going about its daily business, which was weird, because for her everything had changed.

The gunslinger uncocked his pistol, then twirled it and slid it back into his low slung holster with practiced ease.

"Who... are you?" She managed to say, although her words sounded more breathless than she would have liked. "What are you doing here?"

He was sniffing around the coffee machine. "Is this coffee? Think you can fix me up a mug?" he asked. "I haven't had coffee in..." he paused to think about it, and shrugged. His green eyes slid over her outfit in a manner she recognised. He may look like a still from an old western movie, but he was definitely a man.

"Nice outfit."

"I could say the same about you."

"Thank you, ma'am."

She went to the machine and turned it on. It was noisy, but she raised her voice and repeated her questions more forcefully. "Who are you? What are you doing here?"

"Name's Charlie Dawes," he said, leaning back on the counter and crossing his arms. "Who might you be?"

Jennifer tried to decide if that was a trick question, but his motive escaped her. "I'm Jennifer Kendall. I own this place."

"Jennifer, huh?" Those green eyes sized her up. "Guess you must be *the* Jennifer."

Her hands shook as she poured his coffee. Shock, probably. A moment ago she had been pinned and threatened by a thug who worked for Lawrie. Now she was making coffee for Wyatt Earp.

"What do you mean *the* Jennifer? Did someone send you here? Was it Lawrie?"

That gave her pause. She'd taken the gunslinger's actions at face value, believing he had come to her rescue and chased off the bad guys, but maybe it was a double bluff. Maybe he was *also* working for Lawrie. But if so, what on earth was with the outfit?

"What's going on, really?" she asked in her no-nonsense voice that tended to work with lazy staff and slack suppliers.

He shrugged again. "Got me there, little lady."

"I'm not your little lady."

"But that's the thing, Jennifer. You are, and I'm here to help."

Charlie had expected some gratitude, but all he

saw was a mix of confusion and suspicion on Jennifer's pretty face. He had been expecting her to fling herself into his arms.

The little lady was easy on the eye, that was for certain. She only reached his shoulder in height, but she was all woman. Her hair—blonde, always his favourite—was piled up on her head in messy curls and his fingers itched to take it down. She wore a tight blue blouse that showed off her bosom, and a skirt so short it looked more like a bandage, though she had tight trousers on under it, black ones that clung to her legs and showed off every curve. She had ankle-high boots with high heels. They looked familiar, the sort of thing women might have worn back when he was alive.

But that was the only thing that was familiar about her. The rest of the ensemble threatened to scramble his brains. Not that he didn't like it, because he did.

"Who sent you?" she demanded, narrowing her eyes.

She'd given him some coffee in a big white cup with a pink bow printed on it, something that 'Deadeye Dick' wouldn't have been caught dead drinking out of in the past, but Charlie was beyond caring about such things.

He reached for the cup. He was a man who liked his coffee hot and strong, and if he remembered rightly, he'd been suffering while he was here in London. He'd longed for home and the brews he used to have, black and strong enough to take the surface off a dime. The stuff they served had been more like dishwater.

He took a cautious sip and it wasn't bad. Not bad at all. He took another, making her wait for his answer.

"The Sorceress," he said.

"The who?" She looked at him like he was a crazy man, and he supposed that was what he sounded like. "Look, I appreciate your help just now, and the coffee is on the house, but I think you should go."

"I can't go. I have a job to do."

She looked sceptical. "What job?"

"Well, that's the thing." He took the coffee to one of the tables and sat down, stretching out his long legs and crossing his boots at the ankles. "I ain't too sure. I just know I'm here to help you, Jennifer."

"What, are you a guardian angel or something?" she scoffed.

Charlie didn't like her tone so he turned back to the coffee, revelling in its taste. It was close to perfect. All he needed was a campfire and the red dirt and the empty landscape all around him. Here in London, there didn't seem to be a single square of land without a building of some sort on it. The side trips he'd made outside the city, visits to country estates owned by fancy people, were barely memorable. The gloss had soon worn off. Charlie would rather spend time with his fellow performers in the show than sip tea from dainty cups.

"What year is it?" he asked with sudden curiosity. "I died in 1887. How long ago was that, Jennifer?"

He had her attention now. Her blue eyes were very wide. "You *what*? Who *are* you?"

"Told you. Charlie Dawes. I'm part of the Buffalo Bill's Wild West Show in Cremorne Gardens, or was. We played for your queen. Filled the house. You English sure love us cowboys and Indians." He grinned at her. A lock of hair fell over his eye and he tucked it back. He needed a haircut and— he ran his hand over his jaw—a shave.

She came and stood beside his table. She seemed a bit unsteady on her heels; then she flopped down into the chair opposite him. She looked pale and he noticed she was holding her arm. The same arm the no account varmint took hold of when Charlie first came on the scene.

"Eighteen eighty-seven..." she said, enunciating every syllable slowly and without inflection. "You're from a show that ran in Cremorne Gardens."

"That's me. Deadeye Dick." He slapped the Colt six-shooter hanging low on his hip. "Maybe you heard of me? I can shoot a hole through a dollar coin at 90 feet. That was Annie Oakley's trick before I came along, though she never liked that term. Lady was a sharpshooter, no mistake. We teamed up for a bit."

Jennifer smiled and then began to laugh. She put her head in her hands and laughed some more.

He let her get it out of her system while he finished his coffee. He could see how this might be a bit of a shock, but then she hadn't died and been resurrected by some otherworldly sorceress. Between the two of them, he reckoned he'd had the rougher day. But if they were going to be together a while she'd have to get used to the bizarre being real.

"Mighty fine coffee," he said, glancing at the machine where it had come from. "Think I could have another, Jennifer?"

But she wasn't listening.

"You actually believe it, don't you?" she said at last, almost breathless from all the laughing. Her eyes were really something, clear blue, like an Arizona sky. He felt a ripple of desire go straight to his groin. Guess he wasn't so dead after all.

The outside door rattled as it was flung open.

Charlie reached for his Colt, already back on his feet.

A woman stepped inside and gasped. Jennifer reached over to clasp his hand. "Whoa!"

The touch of her fingers on his gave him the sort of shock you might get from those new electric lights, or so he'd heard. He didn't trust them himself. But this shock was different. It felt plenty nice.

He looked into Jennifer's sky-blue eyes as she gently removed the six-shooter from his unresisting fingers.

CHAPTER THREE

CHARLIE DAWES SEEMED TERRIBLY UPSET. He kept shaking his head, even after he'd taken the gun off Jennifer and slid it back into his holster. Meanwhile, she had spent the last five minutes soothing the customer, telling her that Charlie was an actor getting ready for a part in a West End production.

She was fairly certain the woman believed her, and she bought a latte macchiato and a slice of caramel tart before she left. Sugar was good for shock, Jennifer supposed.

"A sharpshooter doesn't let any old folk take his weapon," he said. "What the heck came over me?"

Jennifer couldn't quite understand it either. She'd felt a connection with him she had never felt with a man before. She'd had a few boyfriends, one of them a policeman who had taught her about guns. He had lasted longer than the rest, but none of them had been very serious. With her grandmother sick there hadn't been time to nurture a relationship, and none of them had wanted to stick around when they saw the drama unfolding in her life. And after it was over... well, she hadn't felt like romance. Not for over a year.

Now here was a man who said he had died in 1887 and looked like an extra from a Hollywood western. Her palms were sweaty and her heart was racing. She had too much going on in her life to want a distraction like Charlie Dawes. She already had to deal with Lawrie and his escalating threats and try to keep the Beatnik Café from sinking into even deeper debt. She needed help, certainly, but she wasn't sure Charlie was the one to give it to her.

She should be calling the local hospital, but what could they do other than lock Charlie up as an escaped lunatic? And given that he had saved her a moment ago, that would be an awful way to repay him. He said he was here to help her. Could she trust him? Did she want to?

"Who were those lunk-heads in here before?"

He'd stopped castigating himself and seemed to be ready to have a conversation. Perhaps it was because she'd made him another coffee. He was taking in the aroma as if he might float away on it. She bit back a smile.

"You mean Lawrie's boys? I owe him money. Well, my grandmother did. I thought I had more time to repay, but he seems to have changed his mind."

"What were you doing borrowing money from people like that, Jennifer?"

"As I said, my *grandmother* borrowed from him

to keep the café open. She was sick at the time and probably wasn't thinking straight, but this place meant a lot to her. She opened up back when the Beatles were around." That last part made Charlie frown in confusion. "They used to come in for a cup of tea and a sandwich."

"I'd have squashed them with my heel," he muttered to himself. He genuinely seemed to have no idea who she was talking about.

"They were a band. The Beatnik has a lot of memories that were special for her. Here." She reached over and found a menu, handing it to him. There was a black and white photo of her grandmother in the top left corner, a younger version.

The corner of his mouth kinked up. He met her eyes again—he was one of those people who looked right into your head, and in these days where everyone was focussed on their smartphones, she wasn't sure if she found that refreshing or disconcerting. There was also a keen intelligence in his gaze, despite his laid-back attitude.

"You look like her," he said. Then, as if realising they were talking in the past tense added, "She's gone then?"

Jennifer nodded. Tears threatened behind her eyes, but she had cried herself out over the past few months. Now it felt more like a hovering cloud of sadness that sometimes fell over her. For the most part she could cope by remembering all the happy times she'd had with her grandmother.

"She didn't tell me she'd borrowed money from

Lawrie. She trusted him, we both did, but I think she was embarrassed about needing a loan. And she wanted me to have the café someday. She was between a rock and a hard place."

"You found out?"

"Eventually. When I saw the papers she'd signed, I realised the trouble she was in. They were legal, if barely."

"Can you repay the loan, Jennifer?"

She liked the way he said her name, with that slight drawl and rough tone. He said it a lot, as if the sound of it pleased him, and she liked that too. Then she realised he was waiting for an answer. "No. I thought there was a way I could get some money to pay him, but it didn't work out. I'm probably going to lose everything to Lawrie. I rather think that was his plan all along."

Charlie was staring at her and she thought she knew what he was thinking. She was a gullible fool, or her grandmother was a gullible fool, or both. But he surprised her.

"Hey, maybe this is the thing I'm here to help you with!"

"You mean the thing the, eh, the..."

"Sorceress sent me here for, yeah."

"Why would some powerful sorceress send you to help me save a café, Charlie? It makes no sense."

He shot her a look. Maybe it was the use of his name, which had slipped off her tongue so naturally, or maybe it was the explanation itself that was giving him problems.

"Well, truth be told, I wasn't always the best of

men," he said, looking down into his coffee. His fingers, long and slim like an artist rather than a gunslinger, played with the handle of the mug. "She wants me to show her that I can do better."

Jennifer nodded. "I see," she said carefully, not seeing at all.

"I was always a bit of a lone wolf," he went on.

"You mean you were a loner?"

"I guess what I'm trying to say is, I was a bit selfish. And then the duchess came along and she needed me so much. Well, needed someone and latched onto me. She wouldn't give me up and it made the duke damn angry. That was why he killed me."

Jennifer wondered if she should be listening to this. It was nonsense, it had to be, but he was very persuasive. "Killed you?"

The café door opened again, and Jennifer realised her morning rush had begun. It was a relief to stop talking in riddles with her unexpected and possibly unstable savior.

"Come, let's get you out of sight. I have work to do, and I can't explain that outfit to everyone." She jumped up, smiling, and went to serve her customers.

Charlie found himself banished to the kitchen. He sat at the table for a while, enjoying his coffee and reading magazines of a sort he had never seen before. In his day, they'd had newspapers and booklets with drawings, such as the ones that told of his own exploits. Well, his *supposed* exploits as Deadeye Dick. But what he was looking at now was something altogether different.

For one thing, there was the quality. These photographs were all in color and on paper that was smooth and glossy. And the people in them were all smiling. Nobody smiled in pictures back in his day. You had to stay perfectly still or else the picture could get blurry.

Then there was what these magazines showed. Did men really take the hairs off their body for a smoother look? He shuddered at the thought of the hairs on his chest being shaved off him. And did women *really* read about how to give themselves pleasure with a machine?

He set the magazine aside, having learned far more about this new world than he ever wanted to. The duchess hadn't needed a machine, he thought smugly, she'd had him. And the women he'd slept with had always enjoyed the hairs on his chest. As for his sideburns, there hadn't been anything like them in the photographs. Times had changed, and Buffalo Bill was long dead. First chance he got, he was going to get rid of them.

Out in the shop, he heard Jennifer chatting with the endless rotation of customers, along with the sound of the coffee machine. He reckoned she'd be busy for some time yet. She seemed safe enough, for now.

Charlie got to his feet and went out the back door. The small yard had a tall fence and a gate at the back, leading into an alley. A little stretch of the legs would do him a world of good.

London had changed a great deal, yet he could still see the bones of the city he had once known within it. The river hadn't changed, though it looked cleaner. He walked and walked, crossing the Thames and then back again. There was no danger of him getting lost. He had a head for directions and it was easy to find his way.

Here and there he recognised a building he had seen back in his time, but most of what he saw was new, and very different. He stared up at enormous structures of steel and glass, and peered into crowded shops selling odd items that were almost familiar but not quite. The smell of cooked food wafted out of doorways, tempting him to go inside, while vehicles filled the roads with fumes, and noise. Not a horse to be seen anywhere. The noise of this new world made his head ache.

When he passed a stand with newspapers and noted the date on them, his heart raced. Close to a hundred and fifty years had passed. He was well and truly in the future.

Charlie made his way back to Jennifer's café. The streets were less busy now and people were starting to stare at him as if he was a freak. Someone pointed and shouted in alarm, which was his cue to make himself scarce. He hid down a side street behind a big metal box that stank of old food. A man in a uniform arrived and peered down the alley, presumably looking for him, before he went away again.

With a sigh of relief, Charlie eased out from

behind the smelly bin. He had seen enough. He needed a moment of quiet. He needed to look into Jennifer's blue eyes and remind himself why he was here.

CHAPTER FOUR

ℚ

"WHERE WERE YOU?"

Jennifer glared at him, hands on her hips. When the last customer had left the café, she had hung up her "Back in 10 Minutes" sign and gone into the kitchen. But her gunslinger was nowhere to be found. Her heart had sunk. Had he been a figment of her imagination? She had been looking forward to seeing him again when the rush finally ended. People were back at work now and there wouldn't be much to do for a few hours.

She'd been thinking about what he had said in regard to helping her. He'd certainly frightened off Lawrie's men, but she didn't expect that to last for long. Lawrie wouldn't give up so easily. Maybe Charlie had some ideas for the next time they tried their strong-arm tactics. Maybe just knowing he was here would deter them.

But Charlie was nowhere to be found. It would be a fool's errand to hunt through London looking for him, so she had busied herself with some more baking, hoping he'd come back on his own. A group came in for a late lunch meeting, and had lingered on a while afterwards. It was only after they had gone that she went to check for Charlie again.

She'd opened the door into the tiny backyard and there he was, sitting by the pocket-sized veggie garden where nothing ever grew. One knee was bent up with his folded arms and chin resting on top of it, deep in thought. He turned his head toward her and smiled that slow, sexy smile of his. A smile she found she was already starting to anticipate.

She resisted the urge to tell him off for his disappearing act. It seemed sensible not to let him see how much she already enjoyed his company.

"You've been busy," he said, answering her question. "I checked in, but you were still working."

She sighed and leaned against the nearby wall. "Things should be quieter now. I might get some more in a couple hours, depending on what the fast food chains in the high street are offering this week."

Charlie raised an eyebrow. "Sounds like business isn't what it should be."

"We have a few loyal customers, but they are beginning to slip away now that Gran is gone. I don't know why I'm trying to hang on, it's just… this has been my life for so long, you know? It feels wrong to give in and let Lawrie win."

"I hear ya," he said sincerely, as if he really did understand.

She was surprised how easy it had been to talk

to him. He was a good listener. He was also no
fool. Jennifer made her way to the wooden chair
her grandmother had placed near the garden, in
the hopes that one day the sun would manage to
peep around the apartment block next door for
more than an hour. She sat down and rested her
elbows on the back and lifted her face to that brief
moment of sunshine, making the most of it.

"Where did you go?" she asked him, eyes closed.

"Went for a walk."

Her eyes opened and she stared at him. "Dressed
like *that*?"

He chuckled. "Didn't think you'd be too happy
to hear that, Jennifer."

"With the gun?" She tried not to sound as
shocked as she felt.

"A got a few looks. I don't reckon people see too
many cowboys these days."

"Pretty much none. It's a wonder the police
didn't arrest you."

"One tried his darnedest," he said. He must
have seen the look in her eyes because he held up
his hands as if he were surrendering. "No harm
done, I swear."

"So... your walk. What were you hoping to
find?" Jennifer asked. "I suppose everything's
changed since you were here before?" It was only
after she asked the question that it occurred to her
that she had accepted his story. Or, at least, she
was content to play along for now.

"I recognised a few places, here and there." She
noticed there were dark shadows beneath his green

eyes that she hadn't noticed before. "I wanted to make sure I was really here, get an idea of what I was up against. I wanted to convince myself this wasn't some sort of trick by the Sorceress."

"Why would she do that?"

He sighed. "Can't rightly say, but she's a tricky lady. The way she talks, words get twisted up like a funhouse mirror. Anyway, looks like I'm stuck here with you until I do whatever it is she wants me to do."

"And what does she want you to do?" She really needed to stop repeating everything he said.

"Like I said before, help you," he said, as if it was obvious. "And I'm happy to be of service, ma'am."

Jennifer found herself receiving one of Charlie's piercing looks, the kind that looked right inside her. Right through her. She wiped her palms on her skirt. "That's all very well, but I'm not sure what you can do. I'm in a mess, and there doesn't seem to be any way out. Not with guns anyway. This isn't the old west."

He was silent for a moment. She could see his brain ticking over. "I don't believe in no way out. Just how did this loan shark get hold of your money? Sorry, your grandma's money." He shuffled about, making himself more comfortable. The sun glinted on the star pinned to his chest.

Maybe she could pretend for a minute that he *was* a sheriff in one of those old movies Gran had loved, and that he could perform heroic miracles. She imagined Charlie trading shots with the bad guys, or chasing them out of town on horseback, then rescuing lost children or injured kittens. He'd look good strolling down the main street while everyone gave him admiring glances.

A hundred years ago. Today he'd look rather silly.

Maybe she should tell him her story. Even if he couldn't dig her out of this hole, talking about it might help.

"All right, I'll start from the beginning." Then she proceeded to say nothing at all.

"I'm listening."

"Sorry, just wondering where the beginning is." She took a breath. "Okay. My grandmother was a keen photographer. You know what photographs are?" He had to, of course. She remembered seeing lots of old west photographs.

He nodded. "We had a few taken of the show over the years. Even had a photographer at the Cremorne Gardens to make sure no one forgot the occasion."

Jennifer wondered if those photos still existed. Was there a photograph of Charlie somewhere that would prove...? She pushed the thought aside and continued.

"Gran was keen on photography. It started with her taking photos of the people who came to her café. There were a lot of musicians in this area, and even a few movie stars and models, fashion designers, that sort of thing. But what made her photographs different was that they weren't posed, or in the subject's usual setting. They're intimate. The Beatles—the band I mean—enjoying a cup of tea during a session break. Marianne Faithful popping in for a slice of cake after a shopping spree. You don't know who they are, but you get the idea. Her photos were glimpses of famous people living ordinary lives and they were valuable."

"Worth something more than memories, were they?"

"Oh yes, although I don't think she cared too much about that. When she got sick, she began to let things slide. Payments on her mortgage, the loan she'd taken out to refurbish the café, bills and more bills... Then Lawrie turned up. He popped into the café for a coffee and they got chatting. He said he was in import/export, whatever that means. He seemed nice enough. Certainly knew how to be charming. It was only when Gran passed away that I learned he was a big shot in more shady businesses. We thought he was our friend, but the truth was he'd seen an opportunity. A weakness to exploit. I don't know how he knew she was in trouble, but he knew. Gran said he used to walk around the café, staring at every photograph, chatting to her about old times, winning her over. He may not act the thug like the two who were here earlier, but that's only on the outside."

"What happened after that?" Charlie rubbed his hands together and Jennifer realised the sun was gone. It was getting chilly in her little backyard.

"We should go inside," she began, but he stopped her by standing up and taking off his jacket. He came over and tucked it around her shoulders. It was such a simple and chivalrous gesture, as if it was something he did every day. Perhaps it was.

"Thank you," she said. The jacket was still warm from his body, and she tugged it close around her. She could smell him. Gunpowder and a spicy cinnamon that could be from his hair or his skin.

Charlie shrugged. "I hated the cold when I first came to England, but I got used to it pretty fast. It was either that or freeze to death. You learn to adapt," he said with a smile. "Go on. Lawrie was winning her over. What then?"

"He said he'd look into selling those pictures for her. He made it sound as if it was on retainer, temporary, and she'd get them back after an agreed upon period of time. It seemed too good to be true, but Gran was so relieved at the thought of having some money to pay her debts that she said yes. She signed something and he took away the negatives."

"Negatives?" he asked with a frown.

"You make copies of photos from them. They're irreplaceable."

He nodded. "Oh. The plates. Gotcha. When did you find out about this deal with the devil?"

"She didn't tell me at first. She thought everything would be okay, but then she had second thoughts. When she went round to get the negatives back from Lawrie, he said he'd already sold them to a gallery and handed her what he said was her share. It wasn't a lot, but it was enough. So she didn't tell me, not until the next payments were due and there was nothing left to pay them. When she asked Lawrie this time he shrugged and said the negatives were gone. He made it sound as if she had known this all along. He apologised, said he must have misunderstood. By that time she was starting to doubt her own memory. When she finally broke down and confessed to me what had happened, she thought maybe she *had* misheard. Maybe the mistake was hers and not Lawrie's? I wasn't so sure, but Gran was getting sicker and I was distracted. I wish now I'd paid more attention to what was going on. She was so sad… and I was so angry. Lawrie knew she wasn't well, he *knew* she was vulnerable, and I was beginning to see he'd taken advantage of her. What sort of friend does that?"

"I reckon you wanted to give him a piece of your mind," Charlie said.

"Oh, I certainly did. I threatened to sue him. But he showed me the paperwork Gran had signed and said it was above board. He had a look on his face, not quite smug but near enough. I took it to a solicitor and they said the same. If I wanted to break it or prove Lawrie had taken advantage of her, I would need to spend a lot of money in court. Money we didn't have."

Charlie's focus stayed on her as her voice wavered and her eyes welled up with tears. He was a good listener. "So, all told, she was done out of what was hers?" he said at last.

"Yes. I've even been to the gallery where her photographs are being displayed, but they don't want to know the truth about how they acquired them. They won't even discuss it with me."

"Don't seem fair," he agreed with a nod.

"It isn't. And that's not the worst of it. Lawrie came back. He's a bit of a silver fox... that means older but attractive," she explained for Charlie's benefit. "He's also extremely well-spoken. He got back into Gran's good graces again and this time she borrowed money off him to keep the café going."

"Why'd she do that?"

"She was thinking of me, wanting me to have the only inheritance she had to give. I didn't find out about the loan until after the funeral when the first payment was due. That's when I knew Lawrie had weaseled his way into our lives. I've managed to make a few payments, but there's no way I can keep them up. That's what Lawrie's men were here for this morning."

"Men like that have no conscience," Charlie said quietly. "They prey on the weak, like buzzards."

Jennifer wondered how Lawrie would like being called a buzzard. He was tall and thin but very well dressed, so probably not one bit. But it was true. He was a buzzard in a Savile Row suit.

"The problem is he hasn't done anything strictly illegal," she said. "He acts as if he was doing Gran a favour, and insists she was fully aware of the terms. And now he..." She bit her lip, not sure she wanted to tell him the rest.

He leaned closer, hands clasped loosely between his knees. "There's something else," he said.

"You'd better spill the beans, Jennifer."

She nodded, tugging his coat closer around herself. "There is something else. Lawrie was here a few days ago. He said he could help me, only this time he didn't want to give me money. He wanted... something else from me."

Charlie stiffened like a dog that had sensed danger. His broad shoulders tensed and his face hardened.

"He offered to buy you?"

"More like he wanted me to sell myself. He tried to sugar coat it, saying how much he liked me and wanted to look after me. I can't remember it all now. I was stunned, to be honest. I mean, for him to think he could get away with a thing like that, especially after what he did to my Gran. I told him to get out. He wasn't happy about that."

"You think those no accounts who turned up this morning were trying to make you reconsider?"

"Probably."

He nodded. "This whole thing with your Gran, the photographs and the loan and all that... Seems like it was all to do with him putting you into a position where you had no choice but to agree with anything he said. Perhaps he wanted you from the start."

She stared at him, turning that over in her mind, because it was just... bizarre. And yet she could remember moments where Lawrie seemed to be more interested in her than he should. Little chats in the kitchen while her grandmother was busy with a customer. The flowers that came for her when Gran died. How he had held her at the funeral, his arms a little too tight, and the heat of his breath on her hair. She had pulled away, upset with him even though she hadn't known the full story yet. And when she had found out that he had knowingly done such a terrible thing, it had seemed almost incomprehensible.

But there had been one particular moment at the funeral when she had looked across the room and met his eyes. She had seen the heat of desire in them. Desire and something more. Triumph. She hadn't recognized it for what it was then, but now she could see it as clear as day. The memory made her skin prickle with disgust and betrayal.

"But why?" she burst out. "I mean, he's over fifty. I'm twenty-four."

Charlie chuckled. "Jennifer," he said. "He could be over a hundred and he'd still want you. You're a beautiful woman. Could be he thinks this is the only way he will ever get you."

"Not in a million years," she said angrily. "He's been dishonest all along. But I don't believe you're right about his motivations, Charlie. Lawrie made good money from those photographs, and he'll get hold of the café too if I can't pay him back. If anything, I'm some kind of bonus he thinks he can snatch along the way."

Charlie thought it over a moment. "Where is this gallery? I'd like to see these photographs. And then we probably need to pay a visit to Lawrie."

CHAPTER FIVE

CHARLIE WOULD HAVE TO WAIT until tomorrow to have his wishes granted. Jennifer told him that the café would be closed then and she wouldn't have to worry about losing customers desperate for coffee. Coffee that was, in his opinion, exceptional.

Fortunately, he knew how to be patient, something he was rather good at. A man who could learn to shoot a dollar coin out of the air at 90 paces had to be patient.

She had been candid about her problems, but he wasn't sure what he could do to help. Yet. But one thing Charlie knew about himself, he always had an idea, even when it came to things that looked impossible.

That was how he wangled his way into Bill's show and got himself on the boat to England. Not bad for a poor cowboy without two red cents to rub together. He had been arrogant then, which was easy given that he had nothing much to lose. But as time went on he had more to lose and that arrogance had worn off. He'd begun to wonder what would happen after this wild ride he was on was over. Would he go back home to his time and sink into obscurity?

He took some comfort in knowing that he wouldn't have people wanting to be him, when they didn't really know *him* at all. They only knew the persona. They only knew Deadeye.

But he had touched greatness and rubbed elbows with people far more famous than himself, and he understood that brilliance always fades into dust and someday he would too.

It was a mite depressing.

Jennifer showed her last customer out of the door and was now tidying up. Charlie sat and watched her, sipping his last cup of the day. It didn't take her long to finish. She stood and stared at the cracked pane of glass in the front door.

"I've arranged for a repairman to come Monday," she said, "but I should cover this up in case someone decides to break in. I don't leave any money here, but there's some expensive equipment like the coffee machine."

"Well, we can't have anyone walk off with *that*." Charlie unfurled himself from his seat and came to join her. "Got any lengths of wood? I can hammer them across. Looks like they did some damage to the hinges, too. You might need a new door."

"Are you a carpenter too?" She smiled up at him and her blue eyes were like sunlight on the sea. It took moment before he realised she was still speaking because his brain had stopped working. All he could see was Jennifer's smiling face and the warmth it radiated.

"...something in the shed. I'll go and have a look."

She walked off and he stared after her, probably looking as if his brain had disconnected. Charlie ran a hand over his mouth and closed his eyes.

"Get a grip," he muttered to himself.

Maybe he was still recovering from the magic the Sorceress had used to change him from being dead to being alive, or maybe he'd had too many mugs of Jennifer's damn fine coffee. He took a deep breath and then another, like when he was about to aim at something small in the distance, holding his pistol steady and waiting for the right moment.

That was better.

Jennifer soon returned with a few options, planks of differing length and thickness, dropping them at his feet in a heap, and handing him a hammer and nails.

He chose a sturdy board from the pile and began to work. The glass rattled and threatened to fall out as he hammered, but he secured it with a thinner square of material that Jennifer handed him and kept on working. When the job was done, it looked strong enough to deter any but the most determined burglar.

Jennifer surveyed his work critically, hands on her hips. "I think that should do it," she said. "Well, maybe another piece here?"

He chuckled. "Don't go overboard with the praise now, I'm libel to get a swollen head," he said, doing as she asked.

"I doubt you need any more praise," she said dryly. "I'm sure you get plenty of that."

He felt his mouth split in a smile. "You're nothing like the women I used to know," he admitted to her.

"Maybe that's a good thing."

"I don't know. Without praise, I just might shrivel up and die, Jennifer. Like a plant without water."

He could see her struggle not to smile, but he could tell by the way her eyes lit up that he amused her. That was praise enough.

"You know, I can always sleep here if you're worried," Charlie added after a moment. "Fight off any outlaws."

She looked at him in surprise. "I thought you were going to stay with me," she admitted. He saw a wash of pink colour her cheeks. "I mean, I have a flat across the river. Of course, if you'd rather stay here and—"

He held up his hand to stop her. "No ma'am. I'd rather come home with you. I'm here to help you, Jennifer. And that Lawrie fella might try to drop by your place unannounced."

She hesitated and then nodded. "Okay, come on then."

As she stepped out of the door she stopped and looked up at the sky. "Looks like it's going to rain." She sounded anxious, but he didn't know why she was so surprised. The way he remembered it, it was always raining in London.

Charlie was aware of a few sideways looks on their way across the river. In some ways, it was no different than the last time he was here. The English were too polite to say what they were really thinking out loud. He kept his Colt covered with his jacket as he strolled by Jennifer's side, just in case someone saw it and called the police. He was amazed to learn that carrying a weapon was illegal in London these days.

"How do you protect yourselves then?" he said.

"What do you think the police are for? Besides, we feel safer without weapons."

"Even with those two Lawrie sent to rough you up?" he reminded her. "It was only after they saw my Colt that they high tailed it out of there."

She wrinkled her nose. "Even if I had a gun, I'd be loathe to use it on another human being. Besides, you were a sharpshooter. You did gun tricks. Have you ever shot a flesh and blood person?"

He ran a hand through his hair, pushing it back. "Jennifer, that's not something I'd like to go into right now."

She opened her mouth and closed it again, letting him off the hook. Charlie breathed a sigh of relief. He didn't want to talk about his past; he wanted her to think well of him, and Jennifer wasn't as easily impressed as the women he'd known over a century ago.

They reached a set of strange lights that directed

the traffic. As they waited for the lights to change, there was a rumble of thunder overhead. Their eyes locked. Jennifer's were so blue, and her cheeks were flushed. He knew she felt it too, that tug between them, as if she was tied to him in some way. Whatever was happening here, it wasn't just happening to him.

Had that moment lasted longer, he might have said something awkward, maybe made a lame joke. But thankfully, the heavens opened just then.

Jennifer gasped, holding out her hands as the rain crashed down. Water soaked through her hair and ran down her face, clumping her eyelashes together.

"Oh my God," she said. Neither of them had expected it to come down this hard or this fast. The look of shock on her face was just too adorable, causing Charlie to grin.

"My place is just over there," she raised her voice above the din of the rain. She looked in either direction, but there was too much traffic for them to dash across.

The lights finally changed and they sprinted across the road. Cold rain continued to pour down and the black street surface gleamed. Umbrellas magically appeared everywhere. He could feel the water trickle down the collar of his jacket, and his hair was plastered to his head.

They reached Jennifer's building, and she tapped on a small square board covered in numbers. Her curly blonde hair had turned dark and straight from the rain, and her blouse, visible through her unbuttoned coat, had become transparent. And that was a temptation for the eyes he could not resist.

Her nipples were like little hard beads beneath the blue cloth. She had undergarments on, but the rain had made them all but transparent too. He knew he was gawking but he couldn't help himself. His body tightened, and his cock gave a twitch.

It was only when Jennifer wrapped her arms around herself awkwardly, hiding her breasts, that he realized she'd noticed, and felt uncomfortable about it. He tried to give her a friendly smile, the sort that usually got him out of difficult situations, but she didn't smile back. Her eyes narrowed, and the spark that flared in them had nothing to do with desire. She turned her back and he followed her up the gloomy staircase.

He cleared his throat to apologise when they reached the landing and without pause she started along the dingy corridor. The moment had passed.

Charlie had had his share of bedmates. They were light hearted, fun, and both parties had come away with a satisfied smile. He hadn't expected anything more from them, and certainly hadn't expected, or wanted, his heart to be engaged. Love was for idiots.

This felt different. Charlie felt vulnerable in a way he couldn't remember feeling before. It was as if he was teetering on the edge of something huge.

Then he realized he was watching Jennifer's

rounded ass as she walked in front of him. So much for profound musings.

The thing was, he knew that he wasn't going to act on those feelings. He was here to help, and getting hot and sweaty with her under the bedsheets wasn't what the Sorceress had in mind, much as that primal part of him would have liked it. But whatever he was feeling, that he thought she was feeling too, it was more than lust. He needed to tread carefully.

Jennifer stopped at a door and unlocked it. It creaked open. He followed her inside, ducking under the lintel, and stopped.

It was almost as small as his cabin on the steamship that had brought him to London with the Wild West Show. He might have made some comment about that, but he could tell she was ignoring him. Maybe he should apologise after all.

"I need to change," she said abruptly, pausing at another door. He could see a bathroom sink and a shower stall inside.

"Sure. You're all wet, Jennifer. Might catch a cold."

Her eyes narrowed again. Yeah, he should have just shut up. She hesitated, as if she had some unkind words to say, then closed the door. A moment later he heard water running. Best not to let his imagination go there, he was in enough trouble as it was.

But next thing he knew, he was picturing her lying back in a bath like the duchess's with soapy foam trickling down her neck, her body all slippery and warm. Those rounded breasts bobbing in the water, just asking for him to lean forward and put his mouth…

Charlie shook the thought out of his head and went to the window overlooking the street. He might be getting chilled from the rain in this less than warm apartment, but right now there were parts of him that were far too hot. There was a small table and chair by the window, probably where Jennifer ate her meals, as well as a couch against one of the walls and a stuffed bookshelf. He stripped off his jacket and threw it over the back of the chair.

Charlie ran a hand through his hair and sighed. He needed to wash and change too, but had nothing to change into. He wondered if Jennifer still wanted him here, or if she'd send him out into the rain for daring to admire her womanly attributes?

He didn't think she'd do that, but she might make him sleep on the floor in his wet clothes. That made him uncomfortable in another way.

He couldn't remember being beholden to someone as much as he was now to Jennifer. Back before, he'd always had options, even if they weren't good ones. But now he was trapped in a time and place he barely recognised; there would be no escape until he had done whatever it was he was supposed to do.

He'd been staring out of the window without seeing the view. Not that there was much to see. The rain had turned to drizzle, and his gaze wandered over the street and the crossing where they had stood in the rain, and the tall, crowded buildings opposite. There were a few lights on in the windows, with shadows moving behind closed curtains as the day drew to a close.

His thoughts turned to Jennifer's story about her grandmother, and Lawrie trying to take what wasn't his. He felt a slow anger rise in his chest. Charlie had seen a lot of wrongs in his life and they always made him angry. The world wasn't always a just and fair place, he knew that, but Lawrie's dirty tricks made him furious.

He was so full of righteous anger that it took him a moment to notice the man in the shadows across the street.

He stood in a shallow doorway, sheltered from the rain. There was something in the way the man held himself, his thin body folded slightly at the shoulders, his head tilted to the side as he examined a spot on the sidewalk in front of him.

Then he looked straight up at Charlie, as if he'd known he was there by the window all along.

Despite the distance and the fading light, he recognised that face. That faint smile on thin lips and the short dark hair. He knew him, and yet the man was a stranger. How could he be both?

Charlie stood there confused until an image flashed into his brain; this same man, dressed in bespoke clothing from Bond Street, carrying an ebony cane with a golden tip. Charlie remembered the cold dark eyes from when they were first introduced, sliding over him as if he were mud. He could never forget that look.

It was the duke.

The duke stared at him a little longer, as if wanting to make sure Charlie had no doubt as to who he was, and then he turned and walked away.

Charlie's body tensed. He wanted to chase after him, but it would be impossible to catch up. This hadn't been about the duke wanting a confrontation; he had simply wanted to be seen. He wanted Charlie to know he was here, in London, in the future.

A chill ran through Charlie which had nothing to do with his wet clothing. He rubbed a hand over his mouth, his mind whirling with speculation. How could the duke be here? Had the Sorceress brought him back as well? Why would she do that?

But the duke had been wearing the clothes of Jennifer's world, unlike Charlie. As if he already belonged here, or had been brought back well before.

The Sorceress had to know what was going on. He needed to find a way to talk to her, because matters had taken a very worrying turn.

A voice finally shook him out of his thoughts. "Charlie?"

Jennifer stood behind him drying her hair with a towel, a frown on her pretty face. He suspected she had been calling his name for a while, as he stared at the now empty space on the street.

"Sorry. The mind wanders." He covered up his feelings with a slow smile. He hoped she didn't see how worried he was. He wasn't sure what to make of this, and wanted to consider the situation further before he said anything to Jennifer. The duke being here may not even have anything to do with her.

Then why did he suspect it did? Being brought back from the dead to save a café didn't make a whole hell of a lot of sense. But if the duke was somehow here, well, he'd read enough dime-store novels to recognize when fate and destiny were intersecting, even if he didn't rightly know why.

"You were miles away," she said, but the unasked question remained in her eyes. "You can take a shower now, if you like. I'll dry your clothes for you when you're finished."

"I'd be most grateful," Charlie said, but he sounded distracted. He *was* distracted.

She pointed to the bathroom. "I've laid out a towel and a robe. The best I can do, I'm afraid." Her eyes now avoided his. "I don't have any spare clothes that would fit you. I haven't had a man living here for... well, ever, really."

"I ain't fussy," he said, strangely pleased to hear that from her. "As long as I have my boots."

She laughed. Even that soft huff of breath affected him in ways that weren't appropriate at the moment. Time to put some space between them. Charlie thanked her with a nod and went into the bathroom.

CHAPTER SIX

JENNIFER TOOK A BOX OF eggs out of the
fridge and cracked what was left of them over a
bowl. She needed to shop. As well as eggs she had
a red pepper, some spring onions, a pinch of curry,
and a dollop of cream to work with. There was
bread for toast and some butter. More of a breakfast than a dinner, but it would have to do.

Charlie staying in her flat was unsettling. Especially after that moment they had shared in the
street, and the way he'd looked at her as they
stood outside of her building. Shouldn't she feel
unsafe? He was a stranger who had died over a
hundred years ago. Perhaps the fact that she no
longer doubted that answered her question.

She began to beat the eggs, thinking about the
spark in his green eyes whenever they had slid
over her body, full of a heat that found an answering echo within her. There had been a wild sort
of attraction there she couldn't remember feeling
before.

She didn't have time for this. There was too
much going on in her life to come to grips with

whatever this feeling was between her and Charlie Dawes.

Yet her treacherous brain replayed those moments over and over, as if she had circled them in red and added stars and fireworks. She felt the heat in her blood and the ache in her belly. Even now, she was picturing the curl of his lips, and the dark lashes that framed his green eyes while a lock of hair fell across his forehead. It was as if she had captured it all in high resolution.

And as she pictured him in such intimate detail, part of her wanted to stand up on her tiptoes and press her lips to his. She wanted to run her tongue over them, trace their shape, and slip into the moist warmth inside. She wanted to slide her fingers through his hair and hold him so that she could deepen the kiss, her soft body pressed to his lean hard one...

She shook her head and huffed. Madness, not to be acted upon under any circumstances. Yet there was no denying her desire for him, either. However, Jennifer had a feeling that desire would be curbed in short order.

Supper was almost ready when the bathroom door opened and Charlie stepped out, accompanied by gusts of steam. She bit her lip. He must have seen the amusement in her eyes because his own narrowed in annoyance.

He was wearing the robe she'd put out. She didn't have anything else he would fit into while his clothes dried, and she didn't want him sitting around in a towel, not with her weakening libido.

A spare robe was the best option.

The fact that it was bright orange and had 'Cupcake Queen' written across the front in big friendly letters was just a bonus. That should cool her jets for a while.

A giggle bubbled out before she could stop herself. "Suits you."

"Thanks... I think." He eyed her suspiciously and made his way to the kitchen counter. He wasn't wearing his boots, and his bare feet squeaked on the linoleum. He seated himself on a stool, pushing up the sleeves, and the front opening of the robe gaped. She saw the planes and dips of his chest, strong and lean like the rest of his body, with an additional sprinkle of brown hair...

Okay, so this jet cooling wasn't working out as well as she'd hoped. Under the circumstances he seemed pretty comfortable for such a masculine man. Most men would have felt silly being put in this position, but Charlie had already adapted.

He caught her staring, and remembered how he had ogled her before. His mouth twitched up at the corners.

"Orange always was my colour."

He rested his arms on the counter and leaned in, giving her more of an eye full.

"I was going to apologise," he added, meeting her eyes with an intense look. "For staring. Earlier. Now I think we're even, Jennifer."

She tried to think of something to say, but her brain went blank. She finished spooning the scrambled egg onto the toast on his plate and pushed it toward him. "Eat up."

He stared hungrily at the meal. "I don't rightly remember the last time I ate," he admitted, picking up the fork. "Must have been the night I died. Had some fancy thing the duchess served up. I didn't want to stay, but she insisted. I told her it was the last time, but she never listened."

Jennifer watched him eat. He had mentioned the duke killing him, and she suspected that this was no coincidence.

"Were you and the duchess close?"

He looked up and once again she was startled by the brilliance of those green eyes. There were shadows in them now, holding secrets he didn't want to share.

"Sorry, it's none of my business," she said and turned to her own meal. For a moment they ate in silence.

Charlie sighed and set down his fork. "I don't know what you would call me and the duchess," he said at last. "Fame seems to attract people, and I was famous. I was invited to places I never imagined being invited to, and I met people I never expected to ever meet. I think she wanted to spend time with me because I was always in front of the crowd, showing off, and everyone in her circle was talking about me. Then she got to know me better and she wanted to spend time with me because she liked me. Liked me a bit too much, as it turns out."

"She fell in love with you," Jennifer said.

He rubbed a hand over his jaw and she heard the

rasp of his whiskers. "Maybe."

Charlie had been a celebrity back in his day. He'd embraced it, enjoyed it, and possibly let himself be sucked into it a bit too deep. She thought about modern celebrities who started to believe their own hype and went off the rails. She couldn't really blame him for acting the same way. Besides, he had the sort of charisma that people would naturally be drawn to. She could hardly look down on anyone who had fallen under his spell.

"So this duchess... wife of your duke, I assume."

Charlie nodded.

"Did the duke kill you because of your relationship with his wife? Didn't you suspect he was jealous?"

Charlie shifted uneasily. "I couldn't read the man. He was ice cold. I would have needed an ice pick to chip away at him, to get to his heart. And the duchess assured me that marriage and romance were two different worlds in her circles."

For a moment Jennifer thought she understood what the duchess saw in Charlie. He was warm, sexy, approachable. If her husband was the opposite to that, who could blame her for pursuing him?

"Were you in love with her?" she asked, trying to make her tone neutral when it threatened to turn snarky.

He frowned. The shadows were back in his eyes. "To be honest, Jennifer, I don't think I've ever been in love. Don't believe in it. At first, I was flattered by her attentions. She was the next best thing to royalty, and I was nothing but a cowboy from Arizona. She made me feel important, and I admit I enjoyed that. She took me to places I would never have gone otherwise, the theatre and the opera and big parties at fancy houses. I met people I would never have met without her on my arm. But then she got to talking about us being together forever, that she would divorce the duke and marry me and... and I got worried."

"Because that wasn't what you wanted?" Jennifer said. "Other men would have jumped at the chance, Charlie."

"I ain't other men."

Jennifer was beginning to realize that. "You should have broken things off with her."

He gave her a sheepish look. "You're right, I should have. But, truth is, I felt sorry for her. She was rich and beautiful. She seemed to have everything a woman could want. But the more I got to know her, the more alone I realised she was. At least when I was there I could listen to her, hold her... It seemed little enough. And I did try to break things off, I swear. I even found her someone I thought could take my place, but that only made her angry."

"Oh Charlie," Jennifer sighed. "Of course it made her angry. She wanted *you*, not some stand-in."

His mouth turned down. "I thought I was helping," he muttered.

Poor Charlie. With a sigh, she got up and moved toward the bathroom. "I'll dry your clothes," she said.

He looked up, and the expression on his face made him look strangely vulnerable. "Do you want me to leave?"

Surprised, Jennifer shook her head. "Of course not. You can sleep on the couch tonight."

He didn't argue. He was probably as tired as she was. It had been a long day for both of them. She set the dryer and found a spare duvet and pillows and carried them out to the lounge.

She froze. Charlie was at the sink doing the dishes. It was such an ordinary thing to do, but for a man who had come from the past and was such a, well, such a *man*, it seemed extraordinary.

He glanced at her over his shoulder. "I was taught to clean up after myself," he said. "You cooked, so I clean. Is that how it works in your world, Jennifer?"

"It's supposed to, but you'd be surprised how many people conveniently forget. You know, Charlie, I can understand why the duchess wanted to hang on to you. Did you wash up for her too?"

He chuckled. "Naw, she had a servant for just about everything. I thought I'd get used to it, but I never did." He wiped his hands on the tea towel and instead of hanging it up to dry, tossed it in the sink.

Not quite perfect then, Jennifer thought wryly.

"I used to wonder if she might have been better off if she hadn't been handed everything she wanted from the day she was born. She was bored. She had a brain, and the duke only wanted her around to look pretty."

"Maybe that was why you liked her."

He nodded thoughtfully. "Maybe it was, Jennifer."

She found herself the object of one of his long looks and suddenly felt breathless. Even the bright orange robe with the silly writing couldn't detract from the man's raw sexual appeal. *Damn.* She looked away, pointing to the bedding on the couch.

"There. I'll leave you to it. There's a jar of coffee in the top cupboard. You just have to switch on the kettle to heat the water." She showed him the button he'd have to press, and the coffee jar. "Sorry, it's only instant."

"Instant?" Charlie said warily. "Tried that once or twice. Not a fan."

"Well, maybe it's improved over the last hundred years."

"Maybe."

"I used to have a machine like the one in the café, well not quite as expensive, but it broke and I can't afford another."

He smiled, as if he knew he was making her nervous. "That's fine, Jennifer."

"See you in the morning," she added a little uncomfortably, and went into her bedroom. She shut the door and took a breath, then another.

Maybe she was just tired and needed a good night's sleep. She heard the kettle click out in the kitchen and the rattle of a spoon in the coffee jar. Charlie was making himself at home in her tiny apartment.

For some reason that felt good. Him being here meant she wasn't alone, and she had been very much alone since her grandmother had died. For the longest time, Gran had been all she had.

But she couldn't really complain about her childhood. Gran had always been there for her, and she had friends throughout school and later in business school. It was just that she had lost touch with them, and then Gran was ill and she had no time for socialising.

Hearing Charlie out there, moving about, felt comforting. Like she wasn't quite so alone anymore.

Jennifer climbed into bed and closed her eyes.

CHAPTER SEVEN

THE COUCH WAS COMFORTABLE, APART from a lump right in the middle of his back. Charlie twisted and turned and eventually found a good position. He'd dealt with worse. The Wild West Show had not exactly been luxurious when it came to sleeping accommodations. For a time he lay there, thinking. He had a lot to think about.

Seeing the duke outside on the street had shaken him.

The man who had killed him in the past was here in the future, and Charlie didn't understand why, let alone how. Maybe the duke wasn't satisfied with killing him once and hated him so much he wanted to do it again. He could imagine that, but it still didn't answer how.

His thoughts went around in circles, keeping him restless. But he must have slept at some point because it wasn't until Charlie was in the middle of the dream that he realised he *was* asleep.

He was in the duchess's boudoir, filled with

silks and satins and velvets of opulent colours. The duchess lay on her four-poster bed, naked, her pale skin glowing in the candlelight. Charlie realised that this wasn't so much a dream as a memory.

Once he would have been aroused by the sight of her, eager to give her whatever she wanted. Now he pitied her and longed to escape her cloying arms. He had been flattered by her attention at first, and she had been kind to him. But of late all he saw was a spoilt rich woman. Most of the time, at least.

There were times when she appeared to be genuinely frightened of her powerful husband. Charlie was never sure whether to believe the stories she told of him or not. He suspected she was just playing him, trying to keep him from leaving her. But what if he was wrong? She'd kept him on a short leash and he was getting desperate to cut himself free.

"Where's the duke?" he asked.

She pouted and twisted a strand of her dark hair which shone like a raven's wing. "Oh, I don't know. Out somewhere. He has other women, you know."

"He loves you," Charlie said.

She frowned and shifted nervously in the bed. "I don't like his kind of love. He only wishes to own me, like one of his horses. He wants me to trot when he tells me, and gallop when he commands it. What I want is of no consequence to him."

"And yet here I am with you now. And I'm not the only lover you've taken, I'm sure."

She waved a hand. "He has always ignored my little flings before, just as I have ignored his. But I don't understand his behaviour when it comes to you." She rested her chin on her hand. His eye was drawn to the dip of her waist and curve of her bottom. She was like a sculpture in the museum she had taken him to last week. He could admire her beauty yet he felt no desire. Not anymore.

"He hates me," Charlie answered dryly. It was that simple. The duke might have tolerated his wife's flings with the gentlemen of their circle, but now she had chosen someone so low on the social ladder that was an insult he could not ignore. Yet another reason for Charlie to distance himself from her.

She had a thoughtful look upon her face. "Yes, I suppose he does hate you. But usually when he hates someone he hurts them. I won't tell you how he treats his horses when they disobey him. He hasn't hurt you though, has he?"

"He wouldn't want to try," Charlie retorted, but he was concerned nonetheless. Was the duke planning to harm him in some way? Take a horsewhip to him for his presumption, perhaps? He could imagine that.

In the beginning, he had thought the man a fool to allow his wife to cuckold him whenever the fancy took her, but this man was no fool. Whenever the duke happened to fix him with his cold stare, Charlie felt a tingle of apprehension. He could imagine the duke plotting something horrible against him, and although Charlie was well able to protect himself, he wondered whether the duchess would end up being part of that punishment. He didn't want to be responsible for that. Fact was, she'd be better off without him, and Charlie would certainly be better off without her.

"I need to go," Charlie said now for the tenth time. "They need me at the show. There's some new trick they're trying and I need to practice."

Her brown eyes widened. "Stay a little longer, Charlie. Please. I'm lonely."

"Why not call Bertie? You know how he likes to amuse you with his stories."

Bertie had come with the duchess when she married the duke. Charlie didn't know exactly what he did in the household, but the duchess was very fond of him, and Bertie was devoted to her. In fact, he suspected the poor guy was in love with her. The duchess always said he was more like a younger brother to her, but sometimes Charlie wondered.

"I don't *want* Bertie. You know I don't."

He shook his head. "I'm sorry. I have to go."

She sat up, her long hair falling around her shoulders, pink nipples inviting him, and he wished he still felt the way he had in the beginning. That need to be inside her at any cost. But all he felt was an admiration for her beauty and a powerful wish that they had never met.

"Will you come back tomorrow?" she asked, swaying toward him. "We can have dinner out, if you like."

"I don't think so."

She gave him a wide-eyed look. "Has my husband been threatening you, Charlie? Don't listen to him. You know I despise him."

Charlie wondered how she could despise a man who gave her everything a woman could want. But he supposed he knew. The duke believed love could be bought, and the duchess didn't want to be for sale.

"Did you always despise him?" he asked her.

She picked up a transparent robe and slipped it on. "No. I rather admired him in the beginning, and I married him because it was a good match. You have to understand, that is the way things work here. I thought that one day I may love him, but I didn't realise then that there was no love in him. Only ice water. If I had known *you* then, Charlie, I would never have married him."

Charlie chuckled and shook his head. "You wouldn't have looked twice at me," he said. "I was nothing. This show…" he waved a hand as if to encapsulate London and everything that had happened. "It'll finish and I'll just be a legend in these parts."

She shook her head. "Never!" Her voice raised in pitch. "I'll never forget you. Won't you stay? You can protect me. The duke… he can be cruel as well as cold." She wouldn't meet his gaze. Charlie thought she was playing him, she must be.

Something in him squirmed as he accepted that he was never going to escape her grip unless he hurt her a little. Charlie didn't like hurting women, which was why he never let emotions complicate his dalliances. But this time he was going to have to be blunt. Maybe even a bit brutal.

"Charlie?" she whispered, seeing the resolve in his expression. "Please. Do I have to beg you to stay? Because I will, I really will. I have no pride where you're concerned. I'll give you anything you want, Charlie. *Anything.*"

Now he was embarrassed for her, this beautiful woman with everything, begging for the attentions of a common man who did not want her.

"Don't ever beg," he said sharply. "You're better than that."

"Charlie…"

"I have to go, Duchess. And I don't reckon I'll be coming back. Set your mind to it. There are plenty of other men out there, and you'll find the one for you. But I ain't him. I never was."

Tears filled her eyes, but she blinked them back. Her mouth then curled into a sneer. "So, that's it, is it? 'Charlie Dawes doesn't love anyone,' wasn't that what you told me? I never for a moment believed you were being serious."

"It's not my fault if you expected more from me that I was able to give, Duchess."

The duchess scowled. "I hope that one day someone comes along and you fall painfully, head over heels, in love with her. I hope your heart *aches*. And I hope that she laughs in your face and turns you away. Maybe then you'll understand how I feel now."

"You're better off without me, and you know it," he said in a hard tone.

Tears ran down her face as he pulled on his jacket. Where was Bertie? If he were here he could distract the duchess while Charlie made his getaway.

His holster was on the table inside the front door—she always made him leave it there—and he left the room to get it. She followed him down the stairs, too distraught to care whether the servants saw her dishabille.

He grabbed his holster and buckled it low on his hips as she moved closer. "Charlie," she moaned, "please stay. It's not safe to go out. The duke... He... he said he wanted you dead."

Charlie stared into those dark eyes swimming in tears, uncertain whether he believed her or not. Maybe he should stay? "When did he say this?"

"This morning, last night... I forget. He wants you dead, Charlie. Stay here with me. We can go away together."

"Go away? Where? And do what? Live on what? You need to wake up, Duchess. Face the facts. You may not love your husband, but I don't love you. How would you be better off with me?"

"Charlie!"

He hardened his heart. This was a game to her, a spoilt rich woman's game, and he was done playing. "I need to go." He needed to get back to the show. At least he was among friends there.

"Charlie, no! Listen to me, please!" She wrapped

her arms around him, holding him tight. He had to use more strength than he wanted to escape her grip. Without warning, her fingers turned into claws and she began to scratch at him, trying to get at his face. He pushed her back and she sank to the floor sobbing.

He took a breath, thoroughly disconcerted. He wanted to ask her if she was hurt, to say he was sorry, but that would only give her hope and he couldn't do that.

Charlie turned and left.

He heard her scream in fury behind him, something about him being sorry, but he didn't look back. His heart was pounding, and he cursed himself for allowed things to get so out of control. All he could see in his mind was her face made ugly by grief, so much so that he wasn't taking notice of where he was going.

He was usually careful going out at night. London was a city full of thieves and cutthroats who would knife you for your shoes or the coins in your pocket. But tonight he wasn't thinking straight, the yellow fog swam around him, as he got himself to the Wild West camp grounds. The river was at his side, the smell of the water and the low tide riverbank in his nostrils. He paused. Something was wrong. A sense that had been honed over many years of living dangerously kicked into action.

He hesitated, ready to turn back, and heard a sound. He reached for his gun. Except it wasn't there.

Then he saw the duke, right in front of him, crowding him, his voice as soft and vicious as a sidewinder. "Mr Dawes."

"Duke," he'd replied, trying to sound as if he wasn't worried about the place, the timing, or the fact he was unarmed.

"Your Grace to you," hissed the man before him. "It seems my wife has refused to stop seeing you, so it's time I took you out of the picture. Permanently."

"There's no need. I already—"

He didn't wait for Charlie to finish. He pulled at his walking stick and Charlie saw too late it was actually a rapier. Before he could react, the duke thrust the weapon into him, sliding between his ribs and into his heart. The man was fast; he had to give him that. Even if he'd had his gun, it might not have made a difference.

Darkness filled his vision. The last thing he saw was the duke's cold, satisfied expression.

But his final thought was that this was a sad and lonely death for a man who, for a time anyway, had been famous.

Charlie's eyes opened with a snap. He was no longer in the duchess's boudoir or by the pungent riverbank. He was in Jennifer's tiny flat, and despite the light from the street shining through a chink in the curtains, the shadows were thick around him. It wasn't a nice feeling, especially after the dream he'd just had. Well, memory if you wanted to get picky. It had left him feeling squirmy and uncomfortable inside.

He wondered, had the duchess mourned him? He almost hoped she hadn't, that he had chased off her professed love for him, and she had found someone who could love her like she should be loved. He had a bad feeling, though, that the duke had dealt with her as he had Charlie. The feeling grew as he wondered whether he had misjudged her after all. If leaving her like he did without getting to the bottom of his niggling doubts was his biggest mistake yet.

He heard something move, a swish of cloth, and he sat up, startled, thinking it was Jennifer.

A slim woman walked toward him. Her dark hair was loose about her shoulders, an elaborate gown clung to her body, with a fortune in diamonds nestled about her throat. But it was her face that held his attention. It was the kind of white one only sees on a corpse, and Charlie had seen a few of them in his time.

The duchess took a step forward. There was no doubt that she was dead. Her skin had a deathlike pallor.

"Charlie," she whispered. "I'm sorry. It was my fault."

"Duchess?"

"I wanted you to stay. I wanted you to save me."

"What do you mean?" But his heart sank as he believed he already knew.

"After you died, I wanted to die too, but I knew you would hate that, that I needed to be stronger.

I tried to be strong, Charlie, really I did." She stepped closer, and Charlie could see her head and neck were not quite right.

"But he didn't like it when I stood up to him, Charlie," she said as her neck bent to the side even further. "He defenestrated me, Charlie. Do you know what that means?"

Charlie shook his head, and could see bone protruding from the side of her bent neck.

"He threw me out the window, Charlie." She was almost on top of him now. "He killed me, Charlie. Because of *you*."

He let out a panicked cry, and she was gone.

Was he awake now? He felt around him and recognised the lumpy couch. Just then, the overhead light came on and nearly blinded him. He threw his arm over his eyes.

"Charlie?"

He dropped his arm and sat up, relieved to see that it was Jennifer this time. She stood in the doorway in some sort of sleeping outfit, shorts and a skimpy top, staring at him with concern.

"I heard you cry out. Are you all right?"

He swallowed and stared at her as she came closer, wondering if her neck would flop to the side like a dead fish as well. But it didn't. She was really her, and she was really here.

"Charlie?" she repeated.

He managed to catch his breath, looking at the colourful birds on her nightshirt, a shirt that did nothing to hide her curves. He leaned forward and put his head in his hands as he tried to gather his wits. After a moment, he felt the couch dip and the scent of something floral waft towards him. Jennifer's warm fingers brushed his arm.

"Charlie, what is it?"

"Ghosts," he said. "Memories. The past. I think I was dreaming. At least, I sure as hell hope I was."

He dropped his hands and looked sideways at her. She stared back at him, a little frown on her face. For a moment they just looked at each other, just as they had on the street, and he felt that tug at his chest again. The twist of his heart, as though a key had been inserted and was beginning to turn.

He didn't want to believe what he was feeling. It was ridiculous. He had only known her a short while, yet emotions poured into him, unstoppable, threatening to overflow.

Shit... The duchess had wanted him to fall for someone, to experience the kind of pain she did. She'd wanted him to know how it felt to love and be scorned. Was that what was going to happen now?

No. Charlie was here to help her, that was all. The Sorceress said nothing about love. Whatever he was feeling, it would soon pass. Besides, why would Jennifer want to keep him here any longer than necessary? He'd do what he had to do and then she would thank him, with a pretty little smile no doubt, and send him on his way.

He pictured himself asking for more, begging her as the duchess had begged him, only to see a look of pity on her face, and it made him feel queasy.

No, he needed to protect himself. Protect his heart. He'd always managed it before.

"I'm all right," he said. He knew he sounded unfriendly, but he needed her to go. He needed her to leave before he said or did something stupid.

She got the message. Relieved, he watched her get to her feet and wrap her arms about herself. "Okay," she said, and stared at her feet so that her hair fell forward, hiding her expression. "Goodnight then."

He nodded without answering and watched her pad away. The bedroom door closed. Charlie sighed and shut his eyes, dropping his head once more into his hands.

Charlie, you're an idiot.

He couldn't believe the Sorceress had sent him here for this. She said she wanted him to redeem himself, to be a better man. Surely she wouldn't want him to fall in love with Jennifer only to suffer the same heartbreak he had inflicted on the duchess? How would that help him? It was just downright cruel.

Then a thought occurred to him. What if this wasn't about redemption, but revenge?

He dug his fingers into his hair and pulled until it stung. That was better. He was thinking more clearly now. He had work to do. He'd sort out Jennifer's problems, then he could go home.

Wherever that was.

He heard a click and the narrow gap of light under Jennifer's door went dark. Charlie lay back

on the couch and told himself there was no point
in worrying about things he had no control over.

No point at all.

CHAPTER EIGHT

"I THOUGHT WE COULD GO OUT for breakfast."

Jennifer looked at him, hand on her hip. His clothing had dried and he was dressed again, although the scruff on his jaw was a bit more noticeable. He smirked, as if he knew she was enjoying the view, but she wasn't going to admit that, not even to herself. Her gaze dropped to his holster and she pointed a finger.

"You should—"

His hand went to the gun. "I'm not leaving it behind," he said flatly, a hard set to his lips. "Last time I did, I was murdered."

She stared at him. "You didn't have your gun?"

"He got the drop on me outside the Wild West camp. I went for my gun but it wasn't there. Then he ran me through."

"Where was it then?"

He opened his mouth, closed it again, looking pensive. "I don't rightly know," he said at last. Which was strange, because clearly he'd been buried with it.

She relented with a sigh. "Well, don't let anyone see it. I don't want to spend my day explaining to the police why I am with a man carrying a gun who thinks he died in 1887." He gave her a look and she added, "*I* believe you, but trust me, no one else will."

He nodded without his usual smile and turned away.

Charlie had been quieter this morning, as if something was on his mind. That made sense, she supposed, but there was something else he wasn't telling her, she was sure of it.

His smile came back, lighting up the room. "I won't start shooting unless you tell me to, honest."

Jennifer tried to give a serious stare but she wasn't sure she managed it. "Come on."

They bought breakfast at a busy place near Vauxhall Bridge, taking their order to a sheltered spot by the river. She was warm enough in her red puffer jacket, but Charlie didn't seem to notice the weather. The rain was gone for now, and Jennifer thought Charlie would fare better away from the curious eyes that seemed to follow him. People here probably thought he was a street performer. She just hoped no one tossed money at his feet because she didn't think Charlie would appreciate that.

He watched the pale sunshine as it rippled over the Thames. "Tell me more about you," she said, taking a sip of her coffee. "Did you leave anyone special behind in Arizona? Before fame and fortune called you here?"

He crushed the paper bag that had held his egg and bacon roll in his hand. "I didn't leave anyone who mattered behind, Jennifer. My mother ran off with another man, and my father worked hard every day of his life until one day he was shot dead in a saloon. I was on my own from age ten, running errands, then hooking up with some cowboys working for a rancher. I always had a way with guns, and I didn't want what happened to my Pa to happen to me. I was a natural."

He was quiet for a time, and she suspected he had tweaked his story, taking out any bits he didn't want to tell her, in case it exposed him somehow, or showed her the real man behind the bravado.

"When Buffalo Bill came to town," he went on, "I went for a try out and he took me on. Rest is history."

"Small town boy makes good," she said, trying for an American accent.

He huffed. "As I said, it all went to my head for a bit. By the time I was starting to realize that maybe I should rein myself in a mite. But it was too late."

He dusted some crumbs from his black jeans, and the star on his chest winked as his jacket moved.

"And now you're back," she said.

"And now I'm back." He shot her a curious look. "What about you? Was it always just you and your Gran?"

"Mostly. My parents died when I was young. They died in America. A plane crash."

He frowned, looking at a jet as it flew overhead. He gave a shudder. "Those things have gotta be dangerous."

"They say you have a greater chance of dying in a car accident than a plane."

"Doesn't surprise me, Jennifer," he said seriously. "This world is very crowded." A skate boarder shot past them with music blaring. "And very noisy."

"You get used to it," she offered.

He grunted.

"Actually my grandmother persuaded them to go to America, to try to save their marriage."

"Save it?"

"They were having a rough time, and she believed love was worth fighting for."

He didn't seem to know what to make of that. "Hmm. Perhaps we should get down to business. The photographs?"

"The gallery is in Pimlico," she said. "Back over the river." She wondered whether she should tell him about what had happened last time she was there, but decided to play it by ear. Maybe they had forgotten?

Charlie watched a young woman with a stroller pass by, a toddler clinging to her hand. "Sounds fine." He rose, and spoke with fresh determination in his voice. "Let's go and have a chat with them."

The gallery wasn't that far. Charlie walked

beside Jennifer in silence, watching the passersby. People sauntered or ran, while others sat reading or talking on the phones, something Jennifer had explained to him at length. He still wasn't sure he understood the concept.

He knew about people being able to talk through wires and all, just a step up from the old telegraph, he even thought he had a handle on how it all worked. But these things were more like magic. No wires, could take pictures, moving pictures, even. The television she'd shown him was impressive as all hell, but these phones could do the same things, and you could put them in your pocket.

Shops and cafes were crowded with more people. Life in this world seemed frenzied, in his opinion. They turned up a street flanked by old buildings, old even in his time, and crossed over to a small park with trees. The voices around him were mostly English, though he also heard an American one above the others at one point, and he couldn't help but turn to look.

He felt a little bit homesick, but he wasn't sure if it was for the people or the world he had left behind. As he'd said to Jennifer, his family were all gone. He'd come to London to make a name for himself, and he had. There was nothing for him back in Arizona.

Maybe he was sad for the life he wished he'd had, the loving parents and brothers and sisters. It seemed downright foolish to him now, because that was never going to happen.

Charlie hadn't told Jennifer everything. He hadn't admitted his cowardice. He wasn't sure that was something he wanted her to know. His father was a good and decent man, but with a weakness for drink and picking fights. His father, whom he *should* have revenged.

He looked at Jennifer walking by his side. She was in flat shoes today with bright orange stripes down the sides—she seemed to have a liking for that colour. He was a lot taller than her, so with the flats on she barely reached his shoulder. She was a good-looking woman, and he felt even more protective of her today than he had yesterday. Charlie checked for the reassuring bulge of his Colt under his jacket, just in case.

Charlie never figured he would die the way he had. Well, he hadn't figured on dying at all. The duchess's behaviour had concerned him, sure, but it was more of an irritant. The duke's behaviour had puzzled him more. The man knew his wife had an eye for men, and had always ignored it before. Their marriage was hardly monogamous on either side.

So why did the duke treat Charlie differently from the others? Was it just because he wasn't one of the nobility, that he was a commoner, and an American one at that? Charlie always thought it was more to do with the duchess's partiality for him, yet she'd insisted the man had no love in him. When the duchess had come to him in his dream—more like a nightmare—she'd told him things he'd already half suspected. He was still mulling over them.

And last night the duke was there, right outside Jennifer's flat. Waiting.

He felt a twitch between his shoulder blades that seemed to warn of danger. He needed to be wary, needed to be on the lookout, and there was no way he was leaving Jennifer's side until he'd figured out what was going on.

"Here it is."

Jennifer had stopped outside a glass-fronted building. There was a sign on the sidewalk with its opening hours, and a name: Swinging London. Jennifer pulled open the door, and Charlie followed her in.

The wall in front of them was covered with a huge black and white photograph. Queen Victoria sat in her carriage, her gloved hand raised in a stiff wave to the crowds surrounding her. Recognising her from his own meeting with her, Charlie strolled closer to take a better look. The photo seemed to have been taken around the time of her Golden Jubilee, when Charlie was here with the Wild West Show at the Cremorne Gardens.

Jennifer came to stand beside him. "Someone you know?" she said.

"It was the first time she appeared in public after Prince Albert died, did you know that? They say it was the Wild West Show that tempted her out of mourning."

"I'm not surprised. It was quite the novelty."

"She asked me about the weather in Arizona," he said with a grin. "Said it must be 'awfully dif-

ferent' from England. I said it sure was. She had a
bit of a twinkle in her eye, as if maybe if she was
fifty years younger, she might have been interested in this boy from nowhere."

Jennifer laughed, but her tone was indulgent.
"You certainly have a high opinion of yourself,
Charlie." Then she frowned, all amusement gone.
"It's amazing how quickly I've accepted that you
were around in those days."

"That's because I was," he said, and turned to
look about. "Are there any more photos from my
day here? Might be a few of us 'flamboyant Amer-
icans.'" He was clearly stealing the phrase from
reports of the time.

Jennifer pointed to an advertisement propped
against the wall. "That photo is from an exhibition that's showing at the National Gallery. We
could have a look after we're finished here."

"I'd like that."

She nudged his arm. "Come on then."

He followed her around a partition into another
room. There was a woman seated at a table to one
side, keeping an eye on things. When she saw the
two of them, she frowned.

"There's an entry fee to see the photographs,"
the woman announced in a sharp tone as she came
toward them. She looked like she had a stick up
her ass and her frown only got more pronounced
as she took in Charlie's outfit. "I'm not sure I can
let you in, sir."

Charlie tucked his hands into his belt and
sighed. He'd had quite a few strange looks since

he'd arrived, but this was the first time someone had actually told him he wasn't welcome. Before he could make his feelings known, Jennifer spoke up.

"Charlie is playing a gunslinger in a West End show. He didn't have time to change out of his costume, but he's currently up for a new part in a movie set in 1960s London. That's why we're here. To research the role."

The woman still looked mighty suspicious. There was a badge pinned to her lapel that said Miriam. Her perfume was so overwhelming that Charlie gave an involuntary cough.

"An actor?"

"Yes, ma'am," he assured her with his best smile.

"A Hollywood actor," Jennifer added with her own smile, her eyes narrowing. Amused, Charlie looked from one to the other. The two women seemed to be having a staring contest.

Miriam thawed, but only a tiny amount. When she turned her gaze to Jennifer the ice was back.

"Ms Kendall. I believe you were told not to come to the gallery anymore."

Jennifer stiffened. "I'm here with Charlie. He needs me to take notes."

"Never learned to read and write," Charlie put in, not looking away.

"Method actor," Jennifer added, whatever that meant.

Miriam looked to him as if trying to decide whether or not he was joking. "I'm sorry," she said at last. "I can't allow you in."

Charlie caught Jennifer's hand before she could let loose the fury in her eyes. He could feel her tremble with anger. "Hey, come on now, Miriam," he said smoothly. "Jennifer here is my girl. She suggested this place. So I could get to know a bit about her grandma." He smiled at her. "Isn't that so?"

She nodded and turned back to Miriam. "Charlie's film would put the name of your gallery in the credits," she said suddenly. "I'm sure the owner would be happy about that."

Miriam's gaze slid from one to the other. "I'm not sure whether or not to believe you."

Charlie laughed softly. "I'm famous," he said.

Miriam's brow quirked. "Then why don't I recognize you?"

"He's like Gary Oldman," Jennifer said quickly. "Disappears into every role. Right now you couldn't get him to stop being a cowboy if you tried."

At that, Charlie pushed back his coat and drew the gun and Miriam stepped back with a gasp. Charlie ignored her, spinning the weapon on his finger like a top, then taking aim from his hip, knees slightly bent, as if he was about to fire. "Ma'am, I've met queens and duchesses and even a princess or two," he said, with a grin. "It's the princes who usually ain't so keen on meeting me."

He slid the pistol back into his holster and let his coat fall back in place. Miriam had a hand to her throat. "Is that real?"

"Nah," he assured her, meeting her eyes straight

on. He always lied like that. "Just part of the show."

"Does he always talk like this?" Miriam asked Jennifer.

"Only to queens and duchesses," she replied, straight-faced.

There was a silence, and then Miriam took a breath. "You'd mention the gallery in the credits?"

"Of course," Jennifer said.

Miriam gave in. "Very well, but I don't want any trouble, Ms Kendall. Not after last time. I won't hesitate to lodge a complaint with the police if there is a repeat."

Charlie looked between the two of them. He was about to say something unpleasant, but Jennifer reached out and squeezed his arm. He felt that tingle again, and knew it for what it was. Attraction. But it also got him to hold his tongue.

Jennifer reached into her pocket for her 'smart' phone—which had to be smart, given that it had answered whatever questions Jennifer had given it a while back—followed Miriam to her desk and paid the fee. Without a word, Jennifer returned to his side.

"Lodge a complaint to the police..." she muttered. "*I'm* the one who should be complaining."

"Sounds like you already did. You make a bit of a scene here last time?"

"Hardly. I said some things to some people, I suppose, but..." She cast him a sideways glance and then sighed. "I *may* have made a bit of a scene, but it was warranted."

"Uh-huh. You have a temper then, Jennifer?"

"Only if some varmint has done me wrong," she sang with a western drawl. He smiled, and saw some of the tension ease out of her.

"You won her over," she said. "You're a born charmer, aren't you?"

"And you're my girl," he reminded her. He leaned down and kissed her quick on the lips. Warm soft lips. He had been dying to do that since they met, and now he had.

Jennifer's eyes widened. "Charlie," she began, but he cut her off.

"Miriam is watching."

She glanced over his shoulder, hesitated, and decided to let it go. She pointed toward one of the gallery rooms. "This way."

The room wasn't all that big, but the walls were covered in photographs, ranging from the size of his hand to the size of a stagecoach. Bright posters hung between the photos.

Jennifer led the way through another door, into a squat room with low lighting. A number of glass-topped cases were filled with memorabilia of what Charlie assumed was the 1960s. But Jennifer kept walking and he followed her through another door, and once more the walls were given over to photographs. She stopped.

"This is it. These are Gran's memories."

Charlie turned around. There must have been over a hundred of them on display. "So many."

"They rotate them. She had nearly a thousand.

The rest are in storage somewhere." Her lips quivered and he resisted the urge to pull her into his arms and hold her tight.

"Was she paid a fair price?"

"By Lawrie? Not nearly enough. He said she should be pleased her 'legacy,' as he called it, would continue on."

"And you knew nothing about it until it was too late?"

"I found her crying one night and she blurted it out. I tried to get the gallery to reconsider. I begged Lawrie, but he just shrugged and said it was too late. He tried to pretend everyone had won, but I think his 'commission' was far higher than he'll ever admit to."

Charlie grinned and fingered the handle of his Colt. "You need me to talk to that woman out front? Miriam?"

She eyed him uneasily. "Definitely not, Charlie. You're not serious, are you? You'll only make things worse."

He sighed. "No, I'm not serious. Cowboys don't settle *every* dispute with bullets, you know."

Turning back to the photographs he began to examine them with greater interest. They were set in a period of history smack dab between where he once was and where he was now. It was the distant past, and yet it was also the far future. He was fascinated.

The women of this period wore short skirts, rather like Jennifer's, but without the black leggings, and sometimes with boots up to their thighs. Their hair either hung long and straight around their faces or rose high on top of their heads like ocean waves and their eyes were circled in black paint, while their lips were deathly pale.

As for the men, their tight trousers and pointy shoes and jackets heavy with braid and decoration looked dang impractical. Was this really every day wear? Though some, the ones with long hair, beards and moustaches, weren't that much different from a few of the cowboys he'd known back home. The thought made him grin.

"This is the original photo of my grandmother, the one I use for the café menu," Jennifer called from another display. He went to join her. A younger version of Jennifer with a warm smile hung on the wall. He leaned in, standing so close that their shoulders brushed. He liked being close to her. He wanted to help her and she needed his help, the Sorceress was right about that.

"I'm still using a black and white copy of this on my menu. I don't even know if it's legally mine anymore, and I don't care." There was a fierce look of determination on her pretty face.

Staring at her and the photo, Charlie could see a clear resemblance between Jennifer and her grandmother. Same blonde hair and sweet smile, same big blue eyes. A bearded man had his arm wrapped around Jennifer's grandmother, grinning. They looked as if they were in love.

"That's my grandfather. He was a seaman on a merchant ship. Gran used to say whenever he came home, it was like their honeymoon all over again. He died before I was born, but she still missed him terribly."

"And you miss her," he said gently, surprised at his own empathy. Charlie had a softer side, but usually kept it hidden. He'd learned it was best to keep a distance or else you might find yourself in deeper with folks than you liked.

Before she'd left, his mother was always asking him for money. A dollar here, a dollar there. Then she'd run off with a man with plenty of dollars, leaving Charlie and his father to carry on without her.

Charlie had loved his father. The man was perfect in his eyes, but the truth was he was flawed. He worked hard and he was a good father, but every now and again he went to town and drank himself into delirium. Maybe it was a release from the strain of work and keeping his family fed, but usually he crept home the next day without anything more than a fearsome hangover.

It got worse after Charlie's mother left, and sometimes his father would accuse those around him of being the man she'd ran off with. On most nights, no one paid too much attention. But then one night a stranger took exception, and they'd fought with their fists, and then it had escalated to a gunfight. The man shot his father dead.

In his grief, Charlie had trained with a six-shooter relentlessly, until he was the fastest gun he knew, with aim to match. It was all very well to be fast, but if you missed then you were just as dead.

He'd planned to find the man who had killed his Pa and take his revenge. Planned it for a long time. His father might be dead, but he could still be a good son and give him that eye for an eye justice.

Then one day, he'd learned the man was living on a ranch just two counties over. So he'd set out to find him, and kill him.

When he finally got there, he found that the man had a wife and two young kids. The man had turned his life around and, seeing that, Charlie hadn't been able to go through with it. Charlie had seen the fear in that man's eyes, the pleading, the looks to his family, and he couldn't pull the trigger. Like a coward, he'd climbed onto his horse and rode away.

He made that long journey home feeling as if he'd let his Pa down. All these years he'd promised him revenge, and then, when he could have taken it, he'd walked away. But what choice did he have?

It just so happened that Buffalo Bill was in the next large town he rode into. Bill was looking for performers for his show, and Charlie showed Bill what he could do. He was asked to join on the spot, and next thing he knew he was a somebody.

The show had brought him to London, where he had let fame go to his head. He'd forgotten the rules for survival that he had learned as a boy: take care of yourself first, don't get drawn into other people's problems, don't open your heart.

And yet here he was doing just that, getting

drawn into Jennifer's problems, opening his heart to her. He was a fool who never learned, yet he couldn't help himself. He was a coward who had let his father down. He was a coward who had let the duchess down. How did he know he wouldn't let Jennifer down too?

After Jennifer's tour, they made their way back to the street. Jennifer reminded him they needed to go to the National Gallery, where the Golden Jubilee exhibition Charlie was interested in was being shown. It had been a couple of hours at least since breakfast so along the way, they stopped for coffee and a bite.

Charlie wasn't hungry so Jennifer bought herself a small cake in paper casing. While she ate, he sipped cautiously from his stiff paper cup.

"Not as good as yours," he said.

"You're good for my ego, Charlie." For a moment he lost himself in those sparkling blue eyes again. He caught a blush on her cheeks as she turned away, cleaning her fingers with a disposable napkin.

Something flickered at the edge of Charlie's vision and he looked to the shop window behind her. There was a reflection of a man walking by. Just a glimpse, but it was enough. Charlie spun around, searching for that familiar tall figure.

The street was full of people, but none of them fit.

Jennifer frowned. "What did you see?"

Charlie turned back to her and shrugged his broad shoulders. "Thought I saw someone I knew."

Jennifer gave him a suspicious look. "Charlie," she said, "who else could you possibly know? Who else could have come here from 1887?"

Reluctantly the truth came out, because he wasn't going to lie to her.

"The duke," he said. "I thought I saw the duke."

CHAPTER NINE

CHARLIE HADN'T SAID ANOTHER WORD about his sighting of 'the duke.' When he told her that he'd seen his old enemy she had blurted out that it was impossible.

But then, Charlie was impossible too, wasn't he?

He hadn't argued with her, only shrugged his shoulders and tightened his lips. Those same lips that had kissed her in front of Miriam. Tender, that was the word that sprang to mind. He had kissed her tenderly and she had longed to grab hold of him and learn everything there was to know about that smiling mouth.

Oh God, she was in trouble.

She caught him looking over his shoulder again. He'd done that five times now, and those were only the times she knew about. Did he expect to see the duke following along behind them?

She took Charlie's hand as they caught a bus, trying not to smile at the way his fingers clung to hers. "Didn't you have buses in your day?" she said, leaning against him on their narrow seat.

He turned his head and those green eyes of his

were full of thoughts and secrets. "Not like this." Her heart gave a bump simply from looking at him. Which was just crazy, she told herself.

She turned away, looking straight ahead, pretending to count the stops. But she didn't let go of his hand.

They climbed off at Trafalgar Square and Charlie stopped and tipped his head back, staring up at Nelson's Column. "Who's that again?" he asked her. "Looks important."

"Lord Nelson. Naval hero. You know, Battle of Trafalgar?"

"I wonder," he said, and peered down at her with that intense stare of his. "Are there any statues of me?"

She blinked. "Of you?"

He shuffled awkwardly. "I was famous in my day," he reminded her. "I thought, I dunno…"

"Maybe we can find out."

He seemed relieved. "There's probably one out there somewhere," he said, but she heard the unspoken doubt beneath the bravado in his voice.

They made their way up the stairs of the National Gallery, and Jennifer pondered on why Charlie felt he needed a statue of himself. Was it because he thought he deserved one, or something else? He seemed a simple sort of man, but she was beginning to learn that the real Charlie went much deeper.

Jennifer led the way, pausing only at the help desk to find the way to the Jubilee Exhibition. Charlie kept close, as if he were keeping watch over her. She wasn't sure whether she found that comforting or disturbing, because she had to ask herself why he felt the need to do that. Did Charlie know something she didn't? Was this to do with the murderous duke?

Up ahead was a smaller version of the photo they'd seen in the Pimlico gallery, with Queen Victoria waving from her carriage. Arrows pointed toward a purpose-made room with panels painted soft grey, creating a gallery within a gallery.

She was going to remind Charlie not to be disappointed if he didn't find anything about himself, when she spotted a poster. It had the words 'Wild West Show' on it, hanging over a man with wild hair she assumed was Buffalo Bill. He held two six-shooters.

Charlie had seen it too, and he quickened his pace with a look of anticipation, his coat flapping around in his haste. She smiled at his excitement, and gave an apologetic glance to an older woman who had been going in the same direction before Charlie cut her off.

She gazed around the room at the collection of memorabilia. Maybe Charlie *was* here somewhere? Charlie was still busy with the poster, and Jennifer was tempted to follow him, but this search needed something more organized than a scattergun approach. She was about to return to the beginning when something on the far wall caught her eye.

The woman Charlie had cut off bumped into

her and muttered something rude before stalking off halfway through Jennifer's apology.

Jennifer closed in on the far wall. The photo had been blown up to the size of a large television screen. It was of a man with a gun, and the photographer had caught the moment just when the weapon had been fired. Smoke lingered around the barrel, while in the background a crowd of people could be seen cheering.

Jennifer smiled.

It was Charlie. He stood sideways to the camera, arm held out straight and steady, the pistol an extension of his arm, and his eyes narrowed as he took aim. There was that focus she was beginning to recognize so well, that determination that was often at odds with his easy going manner.

She turned to call him over and saw he was already on his way. "Well, how about that, Jennifer?" he said, nodding back toward the poster they had seen first. "Buffalo Bill Cody. He never let the truth get in the way of a good story."

"Is that right?" she said, only half listening. She leaned down to read the card on the wall.

'Deadeye Dick takes aim at a dime at the Wild West Show, part of the Golden Jubilee Celebrations in 1887.'

"Oh my God," she whispered.

A chill ran through her. She had seen him in the photo, she knew it was him, and yet reading the words seemed to make it real. She'd believed his story before, but something about this photo made it seem like he'd just stepped out of a time machine.

"I remember that."

Charlie leaned forward and she felt his warm breath on her cheek, stirring her hair.

"Do you?" she managed to say.

"Yeah. They made me do the shot five times, but the photographer kept taking the picture late, and the recoil would have blurred the shot. Bill was getting real impatient. He wanted to start the show proper." He smiled. "I'm glad they made him wait. Never missed once."

She wondered if she looked as gobsmacked as she felt. He turned toward her and she could see every whisker on his jaw, every lash around those green eyes. He smirked.

"Didn't you believe me?"

"Yes, I did. Of course I did. It's just... I don't know. You can't just *accept* the impossible, even if you believe it, if that makes any sense. This just makes it feel so much more real."

"I know what you mean," he said, turning back to the image. "It all feels pretty odd to me too."

"I wonder if there are any more pictures of you here?" Jennifer moved along the wall, scanning each image as she went, her plans for an organised search forgotten. The Golden Jubilee had been a busy time for Queen Victoria, and the Wild West Show was a small, if important, part. There had been a banquet with a great many kings and queens invited from all over Europe, and it seemed everyone wanted to get into the act. There were celebrations throughout the country to mark this special occasion—and despite the queen's disappearing act after her husband's death, it turned out that she could still draw in a crowd.

Jennifer had nearly reached the end of the exhibits when she found what she was looking for. There was a group shot of the entire Wild West Company. Buffalo Bill sat in the middle, and around him were his performers. She spotted Charlie straight away. He stood to one side, hand on his holster, legs slightly apart, and a serious expression on his handsome face. Since the subject had to keep still, it made sense that he wasn't smiling, but it was a pity. Charlie's smile was something heart-stoppingly special.

She cleared her throat and looked behind her, half hoping to see him there, but he was doing his own search through history on the other side of the room.

Jennifer turned back to the image, which had a lengthy description on a board mounted next to it. It had a few lines of biography on each of the performers, some longer than others. Charlie's was one of the longer ones.

'*Charlie Dawes (aka Deadeye Dick), a sharp-shooter with amazing accuracy, originally from Arizona. With his handsome face and charming manner, he became a big hit with London society. He was found stabbed to death just outside the show's camping grounds by the Thames and there were questions asked about who was involved. His name was linked to the wife of an aristocrat; however it was later revealed that Dawes owed several large gambling debts to some shady characters who investigators believed were the likely culprits. A wretched end to one of the show's most interesting characters.'*

Jennifer blinked back her tears. The epitaph stuck her as particularly poignant. Charlie had fallen in with bad company. That was why he was killed. Had he forgotten that? Had his guilt over the duchess confused him into thinking it was the duke who had murdered him?

She didn't want him to see this, but as she moved away, Charlie appeared at her side. He took one look at her and his gaze sharpened.

"What is it, Jennifer?"

Too late to pretend it didn't exist, she gestured to the photo and the notes beside it. He leaned in to read. She saw the tension in him grow, the clench of his jaw and the lowering brows.

"Do you believe that? Do you believe I'm a no account?"

"No, I…" she began, then she bit her lip. "But… could it be true, Charlie? Did you gamble? Do you remember that?"

Instead of berating her or stalking off as she half expected him to do, he stared hard at her. She could almost see the wheels turn in his brain. "I was never a gambler," he said firmly. "Can't imagine I could forget being one. It's not true."

"Then why does it say you were?"

"My guess is the duke," he said, with a shrug. "Dirty up my name to save his own. Or maybe it wasn't enough for him to kill me, he wanted to see my reputation destroyed."

That made sense, Jennifer thought. Charlie was no liar. He might hold back about his story, but he didn't lie about it. "I believe you," she said. It seemed important to her that he knew that.

He seemed to relax. "I'm glad. I suppose this means there are no statues of me after all."

"Probably not."

He turned back to the photograph of the Wild West Show. The corners of his mouth ticked up. "We had a lot of fun. I wish I'd known how short my life was going to be. I might have done things differently."

"Like what?"

"Made every moment count?" He rubbed a hand over his jaw. "Then again, if I hadn't died like I did, instead of just living moment to moment, I could have thought about what I might be doing after the show closed. I should have realised that fame doesn't last and I should have used what time I had to build a future."

Somewhere in the room behind them there was a bang and Charlie turned, hand to his pistol, his body blocking hers. She stumbled and grabbed hold of him to keep herself from falling. A moment later, he relaxed as they saw a child being told off by his mother, the large book that had been dropped flat on the ground safely retrieved. It was clear, however, that Charlie was ready to jump at just about anything.

"Charlie, do you think the duke has followed you here? Is that why you're so jumpy?"

He shot her a narrowed look, "I know you think it's impossible, but I saw him outside your window last night, and he saw me. He *wanted* me to see him. I don't know what's going on, but I'm starting to think he wasn't happy with just killing me and muddying my reputation. Maybe he wants to do the same thing all over again."

It would be easy to dismiss his concerns as fantasy, but Charlie believed what he was telling her. Looking into his green eyes, she could see Charlie was telling her the truth, at least as he saw it.

She nodded. "Okay. The duke is here somewhere. At least now that we know we can be careful." She looked around the exhibit. "Have you seen everything you want to see?"

He followed her glance. "Yeah. I think I've seen enough of the past. I need to concentrate on the here and now."

"Then let's go home."

They left through a narrow corridor with more photos lining the walls. This time they were of the queen's large family, and included some of the members of her court. Jennifer looked at Charlie, but he wasn't looking at the exhibit anymore. There was sadness in his face, but was it for his past, the memories, or the situation he was in now? She wasn't sure, and it seemed best not to ask.

They made a turn, finally seeing the way out. Then she felt Charlie come to a sudden halt. When she turned back, he was frozen in front of the exhibition's final image. This time it wasn't of the elderly queen.

She had to peer around him to see what held his attention. A woman's head filled the frame of a black and white photo. Her dark hair was dressed in intricate plaits and curls, with ribbons and jewellery twisted through them. All Jennifer could see of her clothing was a high necked blouse with a white frill.

But these were just details. It was her face that caught Jennifer's attention and held it. The woman was beautiful, her features symmetrical, her large dark eyes staring into the camera with untamed emotion, almost as if she were on the verge of screaming.

Jennifer knew without having to read the accompanying plaque that this was Charlie's duchess.

CHAPTER TEN

THE PLAQUE TO THE SIDE of the photograph told the story he had been dreading. A
week after Charlie was murdered, the Duchess of
Bridlington had been discovered dead beneath her
two storey window. There were whispers of opi-
ate use—the duchess's drug of choice had been
laudanum. The coroner ruled that she had thrown
herself from the window and that no one else was
involved. If the duchess had really come to him
last night, then that wasn't true and the duke had
destroyed her reputation just as he had Charlie's.

Charlie turned back to the photo. He knew that
beautiful face so well, although in his mind she
would forever be the sobbing woman he turned his
back on that final night. The duchess. A woman
of contradictions. He knew now he should have
tried harder to help her instead of walking away.

"She's gorgeous," Jennifer said next to him.

"That she was." His voice sounded hoarse.
"And more fragile than I realised. Already a little
broken before I knew her, and more broken afterwards. Says here that she killed herself after I died,

but I don't believe that. I think the duke killed her too. Hell, I know it."

"Oh, Charlie…"

He looked to the woman at his side, and couldn't look away. Her features, soft and pretty, her blue eyes full of sympathy and understanding. A lock of blonde hair had loosened from her topknot and was brushing her cheek. He reached out and tucked it behind her ear, brushing her warm skin.

Jennifer was real, she was here with him, and as flattering as the duchess's attentions had been, his heart had never been engaged. Now it was.

That should have been a revelation, but Charlie had already begun to suspect that he was falling in love with Jennifer, and feared he was meant to.

She reached up and took his hand in hers. "I'm sure if you'd known what was going to happen, you'd have saved her."

With a sigh, he rested his cheek on top of her head, taking in the sweet scent of her. "I wish that were true. Fact is, I did hurt her on purpose, trying to make it easier to walk away."

"But you didn't love her. Staying with her would have only hurt more in the long run. You weren't to know you were both going to be killed."

"Uh-huh. That's what I tell myself, but I can't help thinking I should have known better."

For a moment they stayed there, enjoying the moment. Then Jennifer gave him a nudge.

"Cut that out. I'm ticklish."

She smiled up at him, her fingers splayed on his chest, and he wanted to kiss her so much. He wanted to slide his tongue into her warm mouth and wrap his arms tight about her.

And for an instant, he thought that was what she wanted too. Then Jennifer took a step back.

"We should get going," she said. Her expression was wiped of any affection, and she moved toward the exit. "I need to do some shopping or we won't have anything to eat."

He followed her out, saying nothing. She was talking about food now, as if their tender moment had never been. "Do you have any preferences when it comes to food? What is it that cowboys eat anyway?"

"You mean out working? Beans, mostly. Chilli and beans sometimes. But if you're asking what I ate while I was here in London, then it was fancy, Jennifer. French delicacies I couldn't even pronounce. Personally, I like steak, cooked. You can keep your *tartare* to yourself."

He'd made her laugh. "Well I'm sorry. I'm not sure my budget runs to steak. I was thinking more of a chicken and mushroom risotto."

"Sounds mighty fine to me."

The surface of Trafalgar Square was wet, as if there'd been a shower while they were inside. Jennifer got him onto another bus, and he felt a little more at ease this time, although the speed with which the darn thing went at was still a mite disconcerting. His fingers gripped the seat rest a little tighter than was probably necessary.

Outside the window he watched the city go by and marvelled again at all the changes. No horses or carriages to be seen, no horse-drawn trollies, and the people around him, especially the ladies, were all dressed in a way that made him stare longer than was polite.

"Charlie," Jennifer hissed, nudging him.

"I can't help it," he said, catching her hand and holding it. "Do people really think it's all right to go out in public like that? I mean, ain't she cold?"

She followed his gaze to a young girl in a barely-there pair of shorts and minuscule top under her ankle length coat. "Just about anything goes these days."

"You ever wear something like that?"

Jennifer snorted. "Gran would have killed me."

Charlie smiled. "Grandmothers haven't changed much over the years, then. I remember mine. She was a firebrand if I did or said anything she didn't consider fitting."

She nodded, and he became entranced by her blue eyes warming toward him. He cleared his throat and looked away before he could do something unfitting.

Jennifer led him off the bus at a busy street and he followed her into a store called Waitrose, which was filled with more food than he'd ever seen in one place before. Charlie carried the basket for her while she piled it high, then carried the bags back to her flat. By then his arms were starting to ache.

All the while, he kept his eyes peeled, but didn't see anyone who looked like the duke. Which was just as well. He'd hate to drop the bags, sacrificing the eggs as well as the rest, if he needed to get to his Colt.

Jennifer tapped the buttons to open the door to her building, and he heaved a sigh of relief as he followed her to her flat. At least he'd hear the duke coming if he broke in, and that would give him time to prepare.

The flat was cold, just like before. Jennifer turned on the heating and shrugged out of her jacket. Outside, the winter sky was losing its light. He examined the street below him, but apart from a couple strolling along with those cardboard cups of coffee, there was no one to be seen.

Jennifer started to put away the food. "Are you hungry yet?"

"Not hungry. Coffee maybe?"

She smiled and switched on the kettle to boil the water. "I thought you might say that. Picked up some of the good stuff for you. We can watch something. The news?" She gave him a look and then shook her head. "Maybe not. I think that might just be too much too soon for a man from 1887. How about a movie, Charlie? One of my grandmother's favourites was *High Noon*. I have it here somewhere."

Charlie watched her go to a glass fronted cupboard and sort through what at first looked like a bunch of thin books on one of the shelves. She slid out one and carried it over to the thing she called a television, opposite the couch. It wasn't a book at all, though, but a case holding a large disc with a cowboy on it and the words *High Noon*.

"How's that work?" he asked.

"Sit down and I'll show you," she said as she fiddled with something. She slid the disc into a machine, and the dark screen burst into light.

He watched suspiciously as she pressed buttons on a long dark device that he presumed somehow talked to the machine she was pointing it at, even though there weren't any wires. Suddenly, music blared out of the screen and he was watching a show.

He had seen moving pictures in some of the shops they'd passed earlier, and while it was still like magic to him, the fact this was in black and white somehow made all the difference. It was as if the photos from the Wild West show had come to life. He imagined that picture of himself at the gallery moving in a similar way instead of being a moment frozen in time.

He couldn't say a word. He just stared.

"Charlie?" Jennifer said, her chin resting on his shoulder. "Are you all right?"

"Huh?"

He felt her body shake as she giggled, the warm press of her breasts against his arm.

"Your coffee should be ready," she said, getting up again. "Make yourself comfortable while I cook dinner."

He nodded, but in truth he hardly heard her; his focus was on the screen and the unfolding story. He did a lot of reading in his down time with the Wild West Show, and he had read about some Frenchman who had taken some moving pictures not long before Charlie arrived in England. But this was so much more. So true to life with smooth movement and sound, and despite them being without colour he found he could imagine the colours without any trouble. Every time there was a gunshot he jumped, and he found himself leaning forward during the quiet moments, listening intently to the conversation.

If he had been there, Charlie told himself, he'd have stood by Will Kane. He wouldn't have been a coward and put his own self-interest first.

Then he remembered; that was just what he had done. Not so much with the man who had killed his father perhaps, but the duchess… Charlie had pushed her away when he should have tried harder to help, instead of pretending the danger wasn't real. She had died and that was down to him.

He tried to shake off his dark thoughts and watch the movie. He could hear Jennifer in the small kitchen, chopping and stirring, and saw her move about in the periphery of his vision, but it was as if he were in another world altogether. Perhaps not a real world, more like a show in a theatre or something put on by Buffalo Bill, the performances carefully choreographed for maximum enjoyment. But it was real enough, and the thing was, it *was* his world. He understood it. He'd lived in a town like that, and his father had died in one.

The inevitable gunfight happened, the good and decent man won, and left town with his brave and beautiful wife.

The screen went black. Jennifer had joined him off and on during the show, but now she was setting the small table near the window and he could smell something delicious cooking. The shape of her was silhouetted against the street light outside, and the feelings he had been holding back since the movie ended overwhelmed him.

Jennifer finished setting the table turned toward him. He saw her frown. "Are you all right?"

He tried to sound upbeat. "I think so. That was… that was…"

"Oh Charlie." She crossed the small room and knelt on the couch beside him, her arms wrapped around him and her cheek pressed to his. He was stunned by the wonderful feel of her. He closed his arms closed around her and held her fast.

"I'm sorry," she said. "I thought you'd like it. Cowboys and gunfights and all that. I thought it would remind you of your days in the show. I didn't think it would make you sad."

"Not sad," he responded, nuzzling against her ear and the soft skin of her neck. Her hair tickled his nose. "Not exactly."

She leaned back in his arms so that she could see his face. "What then?"

"It brought back a lot of memories, is all. And it reminded me about what the Sorceress wants from me, Jennifer. The sort of man I need to be."

He removed one of his hands and cupped the side of her face. He was ready to let her go if she didn't want this to go any further. Instead, she leaned into his touch. That was his cue to press his lips to hers. For a second, he wondered whether she was going to push him away, or have second thoughts, but then she kissed him back and he knew she wanted this as much as he did.

She wrapped her arms around his neck and nestled in closer. He kissed her again, deeper this time, tasting her with his tongue, and it was so good. She said something but he found himself struggling to understand what it was, his mind was too focussed on his raging desire and the way she seemed to want him with the same urgency.

"Gun," she panted, moving her hips as she rained little biting kisses down his neck.

Finally understanding, Charlie fumbled at the belt that held his holster. He dragged it off and tossed it on the couch beside him. She sighed and moved closer. He cupped her bottom in his palms, lifting her so that the soft notch between her thighs pressed against his cock.

Jennifer gasped, her head falling back as if she didn't have the strength to hold it up any longer. He licked the curve of her throat, and then pressed his face against the soft shape of her breasts.

"I don't know if we should be doing this…" she said, and her voice stopped him dead. He really hoped she didn't mean that.

"…but I can't help myself."

Charlie sighed with relief. Then she was lifting his head, her fingers tangled in his hair, holding him so she could kiss him again. He slid his tongue into her mouth, losing himself in the taste and sensation of her. This woman he barely knew, yet felt he had known forever.

He found her breast with his hand, feeling the weight of it in his palm, his thumb finding her hard nipple. She arched against his caress.

"Yes, Charlie," she breathed. "Yes."

Those words meant everything to him; his name on her lips, the permission she was giving him, and the desire they so clearly shared. Fumbling a little in his eagerness, he found the hem of her blouse and brought it over her head, throwing it on top of his holster. He paused a moment to take her in.

She wore plain white underwear and because this was Jennifer, a woman he had real feelings for, he found that far more alluring than all the satin and lace the duchess had dressed up in.

He ran his finger along the edge of the cup, and followed it with his tongue, then he drew the tip of her breast into his mouth and sucked through the thin cloth. Her hands flew to his shoulders. When he looked up at her he saw her blue eyes dazed with lust and her mouth swollen from his kisses. There was no doubt in Charlie's mind that she was in this as deep as he was.

His fingers soon found the hooks at the back of her white garment, and undid them. Now her breasts were bared to him, full and soft with rose pink nipples. Charlie leaned in and feasted on them with tongue and lips and mouth.

He jerked in surprise. Her hand was on his cock, exploring the hard length. *Damn*. He didn't dare wait any longer. Charlie stood up, with her still wrapped around him, and began to walk.

"Put me down, Charlie!" she cried out in surprise before she laughed.

He ignored her plea, and a moment later they were in the bedroom. He collapsed on the side of the mattress with her still in his arms, and his mouth once again found hers as he prepared to settle in.

Jennifer had other ideas, though. She pushed off him and stood, shoving down her tight trousers, hopping from one leg to the other, and balancing by holding on to his shoulder. He would have pulled her onto his lap, but he was distracted by her underwear. It seemed to consist of little more than narrow strings and a small white triangle of cloth. With a groan he busied himself removing it from her. Naked, he needed her naked.

At the same time, Jennifer was tugging his shirt open, desperate to get at his bare skin. Her palms smoothed over his chest. Her eyes were dark with desire, and she bent her head and licked his flat brown nipple as if it was candy.

"Jennifer," he groaned.

She licked the other one, smiling at him through her lashes, and then she fought to get his shirt off as quickly as possible. Her gaze wandered over his naked torso, reaching out a finger to trace the line of his broad shoulder, then down over the muscles of his arm.

"Like what you see?" he asked.

"Lie back," she said, and that seemed answer enough.

Charlie was normally the one taking charge, but he found he didn't mind her telling him what to do one bit. His desire for her, almost beyond his control, ramped up another notch. He fell back onto her bed, still wearing his jeans, and felt her hands unfasten them, then pull them down over his thighs and off his bare feet.

Charlie had always been comfortable with his body. He'd been told by countless women that he was a good looking man, and they'd had no reason to lie, but he still felt a bit self-conscious about what Jennifer thought. Her opinion mattered to him more than it had with anyone else.

He propped himself up on his elbows and watched as she left his jeans where they fell. She seemed distracted by the sight of his long, lean body. Then she knelt over him and reached for his cock.

"Yeah, that's—" he began, only to fall back again with a strangled cry as she licked down the hard length of him.

"You're very vocal," she purred.

"*Lord almighty,*" he moaned as she took him in her mouth, and used every ounce of control to not thrust into that tight warmth. He wanted to push her away because he wasn't sure he could hold on much longer, but he also wanted to pull her closer, go deeper.

Just as he had decided it wouldn't be fair to stop her when she clearly wanted to carry on, she stopped and said a word that caused his heart to sink.

"Condom?"

Jennifer tried to tell herself they should slow down. That was the responsible thing to do. Take things slowly. But as soon as he'd kissed her, she'd melted. She could feel how wet she was, embarrassingly so. It had been so long since she'd craved someone this much, and she had no intention of slowing down. She wanted him just as much as he wanted her. Why deny themselves a pleasure that may never come again?

But it was more than that. More than lust. There was a connection between her and Charlie, she was sure of it. A link that might not make any sense and yet was undeniable.

He was propped on his elbows again, staring down at her. His handsome face now creased in a worried frown after she had asked him if he had a condom. "I don't have one."

He looked so downcast, as if this was all about to end. She smiled and pointed at the bedside stand. "Don't worry. I do. Top drawer."

He let out a relieved sigh and reached for the drawer. The packet was pretty obvious and he took it out, staring at it in a confused manner.

"Is this it?"

"Not what you're used to?"

"Will it fit?" he asked, genuinely perplexed. "I had a rubber one. Had to clean it up every time I used it. Hell of a lot bigger than this," he added under his breath.

"It stretches," she said, taking the packet from him. She tore open the wrapper and wriggled down until she was on her knees between his thighs. Having him watch her, his chest rising and falling, was far more exciting than she could have imagined. Maybe for him too, she thought, because she felt him harden more beneath her hands. She finished covering him, and then stroked her hands over the firm plane of his belly to his chest. She stretched her body over his, enjoying all that masculine muscle and gold-toned flesh.

He took her mouth in a slow, hot kiss. "Jennifer, I have to have you now. Can't wait."

She tangled her fingers in his hair and gave it a gentle tug. "*Shhhh*. Be patient. I thought you were known for your patience?"

"Sharpshooting is different," he groaned.

He reached down and squeezed her bottom until she felt the hard length of him press against the wet folds between her legs. His green eyes were heated, and she suspected her own looked much the same.

"No, you're right," she gasped as he slid along her sensitized flesh. "We can't wait any longer."

He chuckled and she knelt over him, the head of his cock brushing against her. She panted as if she'd been jogging, even though she never jogged. He gripped her hips with his hands to support her as she lowered herself down onto him, letting him go deep and then deeper.

They both groaned.

"I can feel you," he said in a hoarse voice. "Are

you sure this is all right? I can feel... you're so... so..." He wasn't able to finish the thought. Jennifer suspected the rubber condoms he used were thick and ranked protection over pleasure.

"It's all good," she assured him.

Charlie's green eyes became dazed, and his cheeks flushed. "Use me," he said. "Jennifer, *use* me. I want you to use me."

There was something so hot about hearing a man like Charlie say that. She pressed her hands on his abdomen to steady herself, while he thrust upwards. Their movements grew more urgent as their pleasure increased. She could feel her body begin to crest toward the wave of her climax, but she tried to hold it off so that they could finish together. He reached up to cup her breasts, tugging on her nipples, and it tipped her over the edge.

She felt him lose control along with her as she cried out in ecstasy. Jennifer fell boneless across him, hearing his heavy breaths and feeling his calloused fingertips stroking her back. After a moment, his lips brushed tenderly across her forehead.

She found the energy to lift her head and look at him. He did the same, making sure she was all right. She felt awkward, not knowing what to say. It really had been a long time, though she'd never found talking afterwards a problem with anyone else. Usually, the man was keen to leave, or else he fell asleep.

Charlie gave her a slow, warm smile. "Well, I

think I worked up an appetite."

Jennifer laughed as she pushed herself up. "Clean up, then we can eat."

When she reached the door he heard Charlie say, "Can we watch it again, Jennifer? Can we watch *High Noon*?"

CHAPTER ELEVEN

C HARLIE WOKE UP QUICKLY, AS he always did. It was dark and for a moment he wasn't sure where he was. Then he felt the warm rounded shape of a woman pressed against his side, and smelled her floral scent, along with undertones of the intimacy they had shared.

Jennifer.

He rolled over, wrapping his arms around her and pressing his lips against her. She moaned agreeably.

He cupped her breast while his thigh pressed between hers, and felt her lean back into him. She turned and he found her lips, running the tip of his tongue over their full softness. His heart swelled along with his cock. She was perfect, every inch of her.

"Charlie?" she whispered. "What time is it?"

"Who cares?"

He saw the shine of her eyes focussed on him. She reached up to caress the smooth line of his jaw.

The night before she had insisted he shave

before they went to bed, complaining about getting a rash from his whiskers, and he had been more than happy to oblige, and happier still to get rid of those darn sideburns. She'd sat on the bench beside the basin in the bathroom, swinging her feet and watching him shave, talking about the world he now found himself in, catching him up on the main points. He'd listened to her as he ran the soapy razor carefully over his face.

It was a simple kind of intimacy, but one he couldn't recall ever being a part of before. Most of the time with women he was either dressed for some social engagement, or undressed in bed. There wasn't much in between. And this felt like an in-between moment. The sort of thing people did when they were with someone special, part of something real, and Charlie wanted more of it.

She now rubbed her cheek against his as they cuddled in the bed. "I'm not sure this is a good idea." It was the same thing she'd said last night. He wondered if this time she would decide it really wasn't a good idea, and lay down the law, keeping their relationship strictly professional. He was fairly certain that wouldn't happen, and not just because he was protecting her. Jennifer might have her doubts, but she was as interested in him as he was her.

"Who knows what will happen tomorrow?" he said when it seemed as if she wasn't going to say anything else.

She sighed and rolled over, her head resting on the pillow beside his, facing him. He was sorry she had moved out of his grasp, but this was nice too.

Jennifer's voice became low and hesitant. "This Sorceress… are you expecting her to visit you?"

"I'm hoping so. Got a whole lot of questions to ask her."

"I'm sure you do." Then, "Do you think she meant for this to happen between us? What if she isn't happy about us… being involved? Conflict of interest or something?"

"Don't know. Don't care. *I'm* happy about it."

That made her laugh. "So am I."

They were quiet for a moment, a comfortable sort of quiet. A motor vehicle went by on the street outside and Charlie stirred. "I don't rightly know what is going to happen," he said at last. "I don't know whether I'll have to go back to 1887 when this is all over, or if I'll just be dust laid to rest one last time."

"Didn't the Sorceress tell you?"

"Only that she wanted me to redeem myself. She wanted to transform me into someone like Will Kane in that movie of yours. But she never told me what would happen next."

She found his hand and squeezed it. "Why don't you see yourself as a man like that now, Charlie? You're clearly a brave man."

It took him a moment to find his voice. He didn't want Jennifer to think badly of him, but he had to be truthful with her. He sure didn't want to be another Lawrie, lying for whatever he could get.

"There's different kinds of brave, Jennifer. I don't feel I acted right with the duchess. I felt sorry for her, and I didn't want to hurt her, but I didn't really help her either. I just wanted out. I walked away and got myself killed."

"You said today you think the duke killed her too," Jennifer whispered. "Was that because of you?"

"Maybe. Yes. She had no one else to turn to and I missed the signs, didn't ask the right questions."

"Charlie I don't know if you can blame yourself for any of that. Your duchess doesn't sound very stable."

He understood what she was saying, but it didn't lessen the weight of guilt on his shoulders. He remembered the anguished sobs as she lay at his feet and begged him not to go. And all he had wanted to do was get as far away from her as possible.

"Do you think the Sorceress will send you back so that you can make a different decision?" Jennifer asked. He felt her move closer, her warmth reaching out to him. "Maybe save your life this time? And hers?"

"I don't know," he said. "I don't want to go back, but it's not my decision to make, I reckon. It's up to the Sorceress. But what I did... It doesn't sit right with me, Jennifer."

"I understand." Her voice grew small and sad, "I wish you could stay here with me. I've never... I just wish you could stay, Charlie."

So do I.

He pulled her close, finding her mouth with his, losing himself in the warm taste of her. He needed to be inside her again.

Jennifer dragged a comb through her wet hair as she entered the kitchen. Her body ached, but in a good way. A *very* good way. The two of them had slept in, something she hadn't done in ages. Even on a Sunday there was always something important to do, or something to worry about. When it was the latter, she preferred to get up rather than lie in bed and fret.

Charlie had been insatiable last night, and there was something flattering about that. Not that she hadn't felt the same way, or held her own. Everything about the man attracted her. If he disappeared tomorrow she would never forget him, even if he wasn't a time travelling cowboy.

She hoped that wasn't going to happen, though. Charlie had arrived in her life out of nowhere, and he might just as easily disappear again.

But what if by some miracle he stayed? What then?

The idea of being with Charlie, really being with him, brought to life a kernel of excitement inside her. It would be like a fairy tale. *Her* fairy tale.

At the same time, her pragmatic side warned her not to get her hopes up. She'd felt so alone after Gran died and if she started thinking of Charlie as a permanent fixture in her life, only to have him leave…

Jennifer groaned. Why couldn't she just live in the moment? Enjoy herself? Why did she have to spoil it by worrying?

There was a knock on the door.

Thinking it was her neighbour across the hall-way—he often forgot to stock up on milk—she went to open it. And gasped.

"Lawrie?"

He stood in the dimly lit hallway. His expensive clothing looked good on his tall and thin frame, but then Lawrie always looked well dressed. He also looked like a middle aged man trying to appear younger than he actually was. His short salt and pepper hair was speckled with rain as he leaned toward her. She remembered Charlie's talk of vultures, and realized that Lawrie reminded her of a bird of prey.

"We need to talk, Jennifer," he said, his accent as cut glass as ever. Gran had asked him once what school he'd been to. He'd laughed and said, "A good one."

"We have nothing to talk about," she said, and went to close the door.

He was too quick for her, however, pushing it wide and strolling inside as if he owned the place. And her.

"Get out," she hissed. "I don't want to talk to you. You sent those thugs to the café. You can't do things like that. There are laws. Extortion is illegal, Lawrie."

"So is threatening someone with a gun," he

snapped back. "Isn't that what your friend did?"

"He saved me from those thugs, which is more than you—"

He cut her short. "I apologise."

She glared at him.

"I'm afraid my associates misinterpreted my intentions and made a right mess of things. I only want to talk about the café. About the photographs. I want to make things right. I want us to be friends again."

"Friends don't cheat and steal, then try to buy their way into your life," she said coldly. "We were *never* friends, Lawrie."

"You're only saying that because your feelings are hurt," he replied, his mouth curled in amusement. "I simply wish to explain."

His arrogance took her breath away. Jennifer opened her mouth to say something she knew she'd regret when there was a thump from the bedroom.

Lawrie turned to look. *Charlie.* Charlie was in there.

"Just go." She reached for Lawrie's arm, hoping to shove him out of the door. Charlie saw himself as her protector, and if he saw Lawrie here, he might not say something he'd regret, but he'd almost certainly *do* something. And Lawrie wouldn't react well to seeing Charlie in her bedroom.

But it was too late. The door opened and Charlie sauntered out, bare-chested and barefooted. His jeans hung low on his hips, and his hair was still messy from her fingers. His gaze went to her first, as if to assure himself that she was all right. Then he looked at Lawrie.

There was a charge in the air, as if a stick of dynamite had gone off in her flat, leaving everything singed and smoking.

Lawrie's face looked as though it had been carved from granite, his dark eyes full of hatred. Charlie's mouth pressed into a thin line, his shoulders now rigid with tension. They looked like they might fly at each other like two tomcats at any moment.

She stepped between them, but Charlie reached out and grabbed her arm, pulling her toward him before Lawrie could reach her. She fell against his warm chest, and quickly pushed herself away.

"Charlie, wait—"

"Get away from her," he said, staring at Lawrie.

"Charlie, this is Lawrie. He's—"

"Lawrie? *This* is Lawrie?"

"It seems he's worried I might do something awful to you," Lawrie said in his posh accent. "I daresay he should be more worried about himself."

"What do you want?" Charlie growled. She saw him reach for his gun but of course he wasn't wearing it.

Lawrie seemed to notice and his lip curled. "So predictable, Charlie," he said. "But then you always were."

They knew each other? How could that be? How was that possible?

"Get out. Now," Charlie ordered. "Don't come

near her again, you understand?"

Lawrie chuckled, though it was without humour. "Oh no, Charlie, you don't get to order *me* about. But then, you never did know your place." He leaned forward and there was so much malice in his expression that Jennifer would have stumbled back if Charlie hadn't been holding her. "You took what was mine before. It will *not* happen again. This one is mine. I don't care how many times I have to kill you, you're not having her."

Then he was gone. The door slammed shut, making her jump. Charlie's arms dropped and Jennifer tried to catch her breath, shaky and disorientated.

"Who?" she managed. "How?"

Charlie looked as if death had stared him in the face. "That was the duke," he said in a soft, shaken voice. "Lawrie is the duke."

CHAPTER TWELVE

LAWRIE WAS THE DUKE. CHARLIE tried to make sense of it, but there was a dust storm in his head, throwing grit in his eyes so he couldn't see straight. At least, that's what it felt like.

The duke was Lawrie, Jennifer's Lawrie, the man who wanted to own her. Just as he'd owned the duchess.

Jennifer stared at him warily. "Charlie, that's not possible. I've known Lawrie for years. He can't be the duke."

She wanted him to tell her that it wasn't true, that he was mistaken, but he couldn't do it.

"It's him, Jennifer."

He looked to the closed door, torn between chasing after the duke and staying here. This had to be why he was brought here. If he could grab his six-shooter and go after him, he could finish him off once and for all. But that would have meant leaving Jennifer alone, and he couldn't do that.

"You said you saw him yesterday, but I didn't want to believe you," Jennifer said. She sunk down onto the couch, looking small and frightened. Charlie didn't like seeing her like that. Jennifer was strong and knew how to stand up for herself. She had been standing up to Lawrie all this time.

He sat down beside her, taking her hands and rubbing his thumbs over them to soothe her. "You couldn't have known," he said. "Just as well you didn't."

"What, that he is a dead man come from the past?" She tried for sarcasm, but it fell flat. She sighed. "Why is he here, Charlie? What does he want?"

"Apart from you?"

Her eyes darted to his. "You think it's me he wants? Didn't you see the look on his face? I think he wants *you*, Charlie. He wants to kill you. Again."

"He does," Charlie admitted, because he wasn't going to lie to her. "But this time I won't let him. I'm going to stop him. I have to."

"What, shoot him? This isn't the wild west, Charlie. You'll be arrested. Lawrie isn't some spectre that no one will miss. He lives here. He's a businessman, people know him. He's safe because he's made himself a part of this world. You're not."

"No shoot outs at high noon then?" he said with a smile.

"That isn't funny. Charlie, I don't want to lose you. I've only just found you!"

"Jennifer," he said. "I feel the same. I don't know…" He looked up at the ceiling, hoping to find some kind of inspiration. "I don't know why or how, but in the blink of an eye, you became part of me. I think I'd do just about anything to keep you safe."

He saw the shimmer in her eyes as she held back tears. "Then don't throw your life away just to save me. We have to save you too." She leaned in to kiss him on the lips. "We have to save both of us. Understand? After that, we can work out how a man from 1887 and a modern woman can make a life together."

"Sounds good to me." Charlie grinned, glad to see the Jennifer he'd come to know had returned. He kissed her back, his lips lingering.

"Aren't you hungry?" she asked, running her fingers over his jaw.

"Sure am. Just not for food." He leaned in again, and their kiss got hotter and deeper. It might have moved to the next stage if they hadn't been interrupted.

"Ah-*hem*."

There was a blue light by the window, growing brighter, stronger, with that electrical sound that Charlie had grown to dislike. A particularly loud crackle had Jennifer press against him, and he held her so tight it probably hurt.

Charlie opened his mouth to warn her what was happening, but his voice was lost in a sea of white noise.

The Sorceress appeared, walking through the light as if she was walking through an open door, despite the light being three storeys above the street.

"Ah, Charlie. I see you're keeping yourself busy?" It was that same melodious voice from before, beautiful, yet not quite human.

"Ma'am," he choked out. "I was hoping to have a word with you."

"I wish to have a word with you too, Charlie."

Jennifer stared at the woman floating in front of them, unable to look away. Charlie turned her face to his, recognizing that stupefied look. "Better not to do that," he warned her. "Don't meet her—"

"There are *things* in her eyes," Jennifer whispered back. "I can see them."

"Better not to," Charlie said.

"If you're finished whispering amongst yourselves," the Sorceress snapped.

Charlie swallowed and turned back to her. "Apologies, ma'am."

She floated slightly closer, but stopped before he could lose his mind completely. Jennifer stared down at the floor and remained silent.

"I need both of you to listen to me," the Sorceress commanded. "The being you know as 'the duke,' Charlie, and the man you know as 'Lawrie,' Jennifer, are one and the same. He is an immortal."

They both stared at her, and, having caught their undivided attention, she gave a little smile of satisfaction.

"Lawrie is an immortal?" Jennifer said, struggling to believe such things existed, let alone that Lawrie was one of them.

"He is not human," the Sorceress assured her. "Have you not felt a wrongness about him, Jennifer?"

"Yes," she said, struggling to understand. "Sometimes when he looks at me, I feel like a child in a fairytale, only he's the monster about to gobble me up."

"Your instincts are correct. He *is* a monster," the Sorceress assured her. "He is something dark and dangerous, and you must not give in to him."

Charlie held Jennifer even closer.

"The duke—I will call him that because that was who he originally was. After you took the duke's wife from him, Charlie, he was full of such bitterness, such hatred, that it warped his soul. He threw her from the window in a fit of rage. Afterwards, he sought out those who study the black arts to try to bring her back. Even in death he did not want her to escape his grasp. He performed unspeakable acts, but to no avail."

"So he wasn't always immortal?" Jennifer asked.

"No. He turned himself into the inhuman creature he is now, and as time goes on his evil will only increase. That is why he must be stopped."

"Is that why Charlie is here?"

The Sorceress nodded in approval. "He is here because the duke has set his sights on you, Jennifer. He has chosen you as his mate."

"Oh my God," she whispered.

"The duke has two goals. One is to have Jennifer, who he is obsessed with—I do not say loves because what he feels is not love—and the other is to punish you, Charlie, for taking these women away from him."

"I never took the duchess away," Charlie argued. "She wanted out of that loveless relationship long before I showed up."

"You may not have meant to, but she loved you, the lowliest of men, above the duke with all his breeding and power, and the duke knew it. And now here you are again, with Jennifer, who has rejected him despite the hold he has gained over her."

"I don't rightly agree with 'the lowliest of men' bit, ma'am," Charlie said. "And I'm only here because you brought me here."

"I did, didn't I?" she teased, though it was in a frightening tone. "And you have done very well so far. I just had to give you some incentive. However... the most challenging part still lies ahead."

"What's the most challenging part?" Jennifer stumbled over the words but at least her head was up again and she was looking—if not quite at the Sorceress—at least to one side of her.

The Sorceress's terrifying gaze fastened on Charlie. "I am giving you another chance," she said. "You can save both the duchess *and* Jennifer. I need you to smite this evil creature that has roamed the mortal world for far too long. He has an appointment with Sigurd in the Dark World." The serious look on her face vanished for a moment. "You might say the duke has reached his use-by date."

"Smite?" Charlie chose that word—he had no

idea what a 'use by date' was. "You mean you want me to kill him, ma'am?"

The Sorceress sighed, as if he had spoiled her big moment. "Yes, Charlie, I want you to kill him. I have a bullet here that will serve your purpose."

"A silver bullet?" Jennifer piped up, and earned herself a scowl.

"Why do people always say silver?" the Sorceress asked. "No, it isn't silver. Can you do it this time, Charlie?"

Charlie knew that he had messed up badly last time. He hadn't realised what was at stake, or that he would die by the river, be lied about and forgotten. This time he also had Jennifer to think about. He wasn't sure whether he deserved her, but if he could save the duchess and prove to himself that he could be a better man, then surely that was a start?

"What is your answer, Charlie?" the Sorceress asked.

He jumped. "Just lead me to him, ma'am," he said.

The Sorceress smiled. "Excellent."

She held out her hand. Something the size and shape of one of his bullets floated above her palm. "Here is what you must use."

"It looks like an ordinary bullet to me, ma'am."

"And so it is. Remember the duke was not immortal when you knew him back then. He can indeed be killed with an ordinary bullet, Charlie, so you had better not miss, had you?"

"I already got six in my cylinder, ma'am."

"Do you?"

Charlie scowled, wondering what she meant. "Fact is, I wouldn't have been killed the first time around, except someone took my Colt. I reached for it and it was gone."

"Then you'd better make sure that it's there this time, hadn't you, Charlie? Are you ready?"

"You're sending me back," he said, wondering what that would mean for Jennifer.

"I'm sending you back," the Sorceress agreed.

He shivered, knowing he didn't have much time. He looked to Jennifer and tried to smile. "See you around, Jennifer."

"No!" Jennifer cried out, leaping towards him. He felt her hands on his face, her warm breath on his lips as she reached for one last kiss, and then she was gone.

Charlie was hurtling back through the years, back to 1887.

CHAPTER THIRTEEN

CHARLIE FELT DIZZY. HE STUMBLED and reached out to grab hold of something, trying to keep himself upright. His palm stung as it scraped against a very rough surface.

His vision cleared and he could make out the wall of the building he was now leaning against. London's familiar yellow fog swirled around him and he heard the wash of the river beside him, reminding him it wasn't safe to stay here.

There was something he had to do. Something important. There was a stench—rotting food and human waste—below him on the riverbank, a familiar smell at low tide. He peered forward and the fog shifted. He was not far from the Wild West performers' tent village in London.

He wasn't just back in the past, he was reliving the moment that had been his last. The flat, Jennifer, all of it was gone. But he didn't fool himself into thinking she was safe; she would never be safe as long as the duke lived. He remembered what he had to do.

Shoot the duke dead.

A shadow moved in front of him along the riverbank, and grew larger. It was a man coming toward him. The duke. Just like before, the duke was about to kill him. Only this time he wasn't going to win.

Charlie reached for his gun, only to grip on empty air.

The holster was empty.

Jennifer felt sick and dizzy, as if she had been strapped to one of those merry-go-rounds you found in a playground. She took a deep breath, then another, and opened her eyes. She was sitting in a fancy chair in a room lit by sconces on the walls that flickered with a blue light.

Her heart rate picked up, but it wasn't *that* blue light, the one that had accompanied the Sorceress. Jennifer checked back through her memory, trying to remember what had happened, but it was all a haze at the moment.

Slowly, she looked around.

The room seemed ridiculously cluttered. Small tables were covered with ornaments, large bookcases were pressed against the dark green painted walls, and landscapes hung everywhere. The floor was littered with rugs. It looked like a late Victorian era sitting room, and she very much feared that was exactly what it was.

Jennifer tried to stand, only to stop as she felt a tight constriction around her waist. She looked down at what she was wearing. That's when things got *really* weird.

She wore a flaring skirt with elaborate ruching that reached all the way down to the floor. The dress nipped in at her waist, and there must have been some sort of corset, because her waist had never been that small. She was already struggling to breathe. A blue bodice was hooked up in the front, covered with a plague of bows and little lacey caps on the shoulders that could have been called sleeves.

Worst of all, she had a bustle. A great swath of cream satin attached to her bum, and a train that was certain to trip her up.

With shaky hands, she reached up to her hair, only to stop as she noticed that she was holding a fan in one of her hands. She set it aside and reached up again. Her hair was in a topknot, which was at least a little familiar, but there was also what felt like a silk flower fixed up there. She also wore heavy drop earrings and a pearl necklace around her throat.

Jennifer was dressed like a late Victorian lady, as if she belonged in the room.

She got to her feet and tottered a few steps, only to have the bustle and train throw out her balance. She grabbed hold of as much of the skirt as she could and lifted it up. Better. She made her way to the door and peered out, wondering where the hell the Sorceress had sent her. The truth was, she had an uncomfortable feeling she knew *exactly* where.

There was a landing with a gallery and more

lights on the wall, flickering and spitting. She was
about to venture out when she heard a scream,
followed by anguished sobbing.

Jennifer hurried toward the gallery, leaning over
the balustrade to look into the marbled hall below.
Jennifer swallowed hard. Charlie and the duchess
were down there. He was strapping on his belt
and holster, his shoulders held in that tight way
that meant he was feeling stressed. The woman
was almost naked, only a transparent silken thing
about her body, and her dark hair fell loose around
her shoulders.

The duchess threw herself at Charlie, arms flail-
ing, fighting him. He held her back, but she was
either desperate or unhinged. Maybe both. They
struggled a moment longer and then she dropped
to the floor and began to sob.

Charlie barely looked back at her, as if he didn't
want to see her. He appeared shaken, and Jennifer remembered how, when he had told her about
this moment, he felt he should have stayed. She
could see now why he didn't want to. The woman
was inconsolable and irrational. Anything he said
now would only make things worse.

She watched him walk out of the house, the
door closing after him.

A grand staircase led down to the hall, and Jennifer descended it. She asked herself why she was
here. This was Charlie's second chance, not hers.
That the Sorceress had some kind of plan was
obvious, but what was it?

She reached the bottom of the stairs. The duchess hadn't seen her yet. She was on her feet and running toward the door, holding something in her hands.

It was Charlie's Colt.

Jennifer gasped. That was why Charlie hadn't had his gun when the duke ambushed him.

The duchess was fumbling with the gun, and Jennifer realised she was shaking the bullets out into her hand. Then she flung them out into the night.

"No!"

Jennifer's cry brought the duchess around to face her. Her eyes were wet with tears, her mouth swollen, yet she was still beautiful. It was quite depressing to think that anyone could look that good after crying so hard.

"So if you can't have him no one can, is that how it works?" Jennifer asked.

The woman started, as if she hadn't been sure whether Jennifer was real until now. She clutched the empty gun to her bosom. "Who are you?"

Jennifer stopped a few paces away. She had seen her in action and didn't want to get scratched. The duchess was a head taller than her, but Jennifer felt sure she could take her if she had to.

"I'm a friend of Charlie's," she said. "Which is more than I can say about you. Why did you take his gun?"

The duchess shook her head. Tears overflowed in her dark eyes and ran down her cheeks. "He left me," she whispered. "He abandoned me. I thought maybe if I took his gun he'd come back for it…"

"Then why throw the bullets away?"

"Because I…" she didn't finish her thought, but Jennifer thought she knew why. The duchess was afraid *she* might use the gun if she didn't, either on Charlie or herself.

"You know you can't force someone to stay with you if they don't want to," Jennifer said, trying to sound reasonable. "It doesn't work."

"If that were true, I wouldn't be trapped in this marriage." She stared hard at Jennifer. "Charlie has always stayed before. But this time…" Her chin wobbled.

"Do you realise he is going to die and it will be down to you and your husband?" Jennifer said. "Is that what you want? Do you want him to die? Do you want the duke to stab him through the heart?"

The woman raised her chin defiantly. "Why should I care?" she answered. "He doesn't want me."

"No, he doesn't. But he didn't want to hurt you, either. Because he *does* care. He's a good man, a kind man, and you just sent him out to die."

She shook her head, but Jennifer could see the distress in her eyes. "I don't know what to do."

"Give me the gun," Jennifer ordered, using her most authoritarian voice. The duchess looked like the sort who was used to being told what to do, at least she hoped that was the case.

The duchess stared hard at Jennifer. "Who *are* you?" she demanded. "Charlie has never mentioned you."

"He didn't know me until after you were gone. I came later. But then I got sent back."

The duchess cocked her head. "What?"

"No time to explain." She held out her hand. "Gun."

The duchess reluctantly laid the weapon across Jennifer's palm.

"Thank you," she said, breathing a sigh of relief. It was heavier than it looked, but she had used a pistol before. Her old cop boyfriend had made sure she was comfortable around firearms.

"Now, where is your husband?"

"I think he's waiting for Charlie outside the western camp," the duchess wailed, more tears sheening her face. There seemed to be an endless supply. "He said he was going to deal with him, but I only thought he meant to hurt him. He likes to hurt people. I tried to warn Charlie, but then he said he was leaving me, and… I don't want him to die!"

"Then don't let him die. Come on, show me where Charlie lives and we'll save him. That's what you want, isn't it?" The duchess might be a woman scorned, but if she loved Charlie she would not want him to die. Not really.

The duchess moved toward the door and Jennifer grabbed hold of her arm. "Wait! You can't go out like that," she said. "You'll need to dress."

The duchess looked about uncertainly. "I can't dress without my maid."

"Oh my God, we haven't got *time* for that! It'll

be too late! Just throw on a coat or something!"

The woman bit her lip and then drew a deep breath. Her eyes sharpened. "Bertie!" she shouted, which made Jennifer jump.

A young man appeared from nowhere, and bowed low. "Your Grace, how can I serve?" The man had the thickest cockney accent Jennifer had ever heard, even in the movies.

"Take this person to Charlie's camp," she instructed him. "You know where that is."

Bertie looked at the duchess curiously, his eyes remaining on her face rather than her obvious nakedness. But there was a pink hue flooding his cheeks that suggested he was very much aware of what he was trying very hard not to look at.

"Is that what you wish, Your Grace?"

"Yes, yes! Now hurry!"

Bertie beckoned for Jennifer to follow him. She was at the door when she remembered something, and turned back to face the duchess. The woman stood watching them go, looking particularly tragic in her dishabille.

"Listen, I know things seem awful right now. But you have to believe me, you can always find a way out of a difficult situation. Don't let circumstance drag you down. Even if I can't stop your husband... just stay away from any window for a while. Promise me that, okay?"

The duchess frowned, then there was a flicker of humour in her beautiful face "I promise."

Jennifer nodded, then followed Bertie into the night.

CHAPTER FOURTEEN

B ERTIE WASTED NO TIME. HE had the coach brought around and gave the driver their destination, and then climbed aboard with Jennifer.

Late Victorian London was very different from the modern version she inhabited. The fog, for one thing. She had heard about the London fog, anyone who lived here had. She had seen enough Sherlock Holmes to appreciate the idea of how dense it once was, but now that she was actually in it, no movie or book could truly capture the suffocating quality of it, or the sour chemical smell in the air.

"So where are we going, Bertie?"

"Not far now," Bertie assured her. "The duke had me follow Charlie so I know exactly where he will most likely strike. He's a right crafty one," he added darkly. "I only wish I could have taken the duchess away from him, somewhere safe. The duke is a powerful man, and dangerous. She deserves better."

It sounded like Bertie had a crush. "I'm sure she does."

The coach came to a halt and they stepped down. The fog was everywhere. She understood now why such things had been called a pea souper, because it was thick and nasty.

"Which way?" she asked, trying not to cough. She wasn't really dressed for this, but there was no time to think of that now. She had to find Charlie. This was his last chance. If he died again it was doubtful he would get another.

"This way! It's quicker if we go by foot." Bertie stepped up his pace and Jennifer groaned, half jogging in her dreadfully awkward outfit. She almost fell once, and was only saved by Bertie's strong grip at the last moment.

She still had the gun, but it would do no good with an empty cylinder. Charlie had the only bullet, something the Sorceress must have known would happen. The question was, would she reach him in time to save him?

"Here," Bertie said, and she looked up. They were at the river now and Jennifer wanted to hold her nose. The fog swirled around them, making strange shapes, and she caught the muffled sound of voices ahead.

The air cleared enough for her to see two men. She recognised Charlie, even though his back was to her. He staggered, and for a moment she feared she was too late. Then he straightened, and behind him she saw the tall thin shape of the duke.

Lawrie.

She saw the glint of a rapier, and Charlie jerked sideways with a harsh cry.

"No!"

Jennifer's sudden appearance startled the duke into moving back. She put her arms about Charlie as he staggered and leaned against her. She tried to keep him up, but he was so much bigger than her.

Bertie was shouting, distracting the duke, giving her the chance she needed.

"Charlie, where is the bullet? Charlie, *please…*" She thought he was beyond hearing her, but he began to rally, scrabbling at his pocket.

"The gun," he panted. She handed it to him, and saw him load the pistol with grim intent.

The duke, realising what was happening, now charged at them as Charlie raised his gun. He pulled away from her, standing straight, aiming true. And fired.

The noise was deafening and the smell of gunpowder stung her nose. Charlie fell to his knees. She grabbed him again, and he collapsed in her arms on the filthy ground.

Bertie hurried over. The ringing in her ears had passed enough for her to understand what he was saying.

"You killed him," he muttered in awe. "He's stone dead."

Lawrie, the duke, was dead. She couldn't be sorry about that, not after what he'd done to so many people, and what he would have done, had he become the immortal he intended. The world was a better place without him.

Charlie lay limp against her, and she feared that he was dead as well. There was a sticky patch on his shirt that had to be blood. She tried to lift his head from her shoulder and he murmured something. He was alive! But for how long?

"We need help," she said faintly. "Bertie, can you get the coach so we can take him to a doctor?"

The young man hesitated and then he took off, his steps soon swallowed by the dense fog. Jennifer stayed behind holding Charlie—the man she loved.

She wasn't sure when she realised the fog had taken on an electric blue tinge, but she knew what it meant.

"Jennifer," that mysterious voice echoed around them.

A sob rose in her chest. "He's dead, isn't he?"

"He can be saved," the Sorceress assured her. "But I have come for you. I must take you home. Come."

Jennifer stared at her. "Home?"

"To your own time."

Jennifer thought of her café, of her flat, of her loneliness. She looked at Charlie. She couldn't seem to get her thoughts together.

"If you don't come now, you will be trapped here forever," the Sorceress said. "There are things even I cannot change."

Forever with Charlie. What had Gran always said? Love is worth fighting for? Jennifer loved Charlie, there would never be anyone else she connected with so perfectly. She couldn't leave him. She shook her head. "I have to be here for him."

The Sorceress laughed in that soft and rather terrifying way of hers, and then faded from view. "Very well."

Jennifer sat with Charlie, holding him tight against her, praying she had made the right decision.

CHAPTER FIFTEEN

CHARLIE WAS RESTING IN ONE of the tents that had been erected for the Wild West Company performers. He had a makeshift bed that was somehow more uncomfortable than Jennifer's couch, making him grimace in pain.

His injury was better than it had been last week. Every day he recovered a little more, and he was grateful for that. The doc said the blade had just missed hitting any vital organs or arteries, but that he needed to keep his feet up for a while yet.

But Charlie didn't want to lay back and do nothing. He wanted to start work again with the Wild West Show, but Buffalo Bill said he wasn't ready yet. And anyway, Bill wasn't very pleased with him right now.

Charlie remembered the duke stabbing him. He remembered Jennifer handing him his Colt so that he could do what he had come back to do. After that, it was all a bit blurry, though he did recall hearing Jennifer speak to the Sorceress, refusing to leave him.

Jennifer had turned her back on everything she

knew to remain with him. The thought still took his breath away. There had been times during his recuperation when he wondered if she regretted it.

He'd barely seen her since the night the coach had brought him to the doctor, half dead. It wasn't considered proper in these parts for a single man and a single lady to be alone together without some sort of chaperone. He'd seen Jennifer trying not to smile when that was put to her by some of the women in her new circle.

"I'm sure Mr. Dawes is a *perfect* gentleman," she had responded with a coy glance.

"Oh, I'm perfect, alright," he'd retorted.

The duchess had been there too. Charlie wasn't sure what to make of the way she had taken Jennifer under her wing. He'd been suspicious at first, but it turned out they had become fast friends. Stranger things had happened, he supposed, and his life to date had certainly been strange.

He knew that the circumstances surrounding the Duke of Bridlington's death were still being talked about. After Bertie returned with the coach for Charlie, and acting under the duchess's instructions, he had taken the duke's body up onto Hampstead Heath, the scene of many a duelling mishap.

There were rumours that the duke had been involved in some tryst with a married woman whose husband took exception.

Charlie's injury had been explained by Buffalo Bill as an 'accident' during rehearsals, but Charlie knew his days at the show were now numbered. Bill didn't like trouble. So although Charlie's name had been mentioned in regard to the duke's death so had several other men. The duchess had remained stoic through it all, according to Bertie, although she did not particularly enjoy wearing black. Charlie found himself smiling at that.

The tent flap opened, bringing him out of his daydreams. He could hear the Wild West Company practising their famous frontier battle scene outside, with a great many Indian woops and gunfire. Jennifer walked inside and closed the flap behind her.

"You look better," she said, looking him over.

"I feel fine. Bill still won't let me in the show, though."

"He's just protecting his star performer." She came close, her skirts swishing on the floor. He wondered if he would ever get used to seeing her wearing the fashions of his time. He preferred that small skirt and tight leggings that she'd worn the first day he'd seen her, but he comforted himself with the thought that underneath the clothing she was the same woman he had held in his arms, and then some.

She smiled as if reading his mind.

"Should you be here all alone with me, a single gentleman?" he said, teasing her.

"I snuck away," she admitted. Then, "You *are* fine, aren't you? I've been so worried, Charlie."

He reached out a hand and she slipped hers into it. "We did what the Sorceress asked," he said, drawing her close, until she leaned against the bed. "And both of us are here together."

Jennifer sighed and his heart sank. Here it came. She wanted to go home. She hated it here. She…

"Charlie, what am I going to *do* here?" she asked, sinking onto the side of the bed, irritably pushing aside her miles of skirts. "The duchess wants me to sit and drink tea with her guests, and I *hate* it. I'm used to working. I want to run my own life, my own shop. I want to bake fancy cupcakes and chat to my customers."

Charlie bit his lip. The thought of the duchess and Jennifer together, drinking tea, made him chuckle. "She admires you," he said. "I'm grateful for that. When I was recovering here, I was worried about you. I couldn't have protected you."

"She has been generous," Jennifer admitted with a sigh. "It's just that I'm used to being in charge of my own life."

He pushed himself up, wincing at the mild ache, and sat beside her. "Why don't you start up a tea shop?" he said. "Or a coffee shop? I can fund it. I've got money tucked away, and I make enough to keep us going."

She frowned. "A coffee shop?"

"In the King's Road," he said.

She stared at him, eyes wide, as if she had remembered something important. "Gran used to say there was a coffee shop on the site of the Beatnik Café. She told me that she'd felt at home as soon as she opened the door. You don't think…?"

"Why not? Anything's possible."

She smiled, her face lighting up, and he leaned forward and kissed her.

"I love you."

Jennifer rested her head on his shoulder. "I love you too, Charlie," she said with a contented sigh.

"Well, that's good." He straightened up, suddenly full of purpose. "Because I want to get married as soon as possible. When the Wild West Show moves on, I'll have to find other work around here. I have savings, though. Always been more careful with my money than people realise."

"Don't you want to go home?" she asked. "I mean, don't you miss America?"

He thought a moment. "Not enough to go back. We'll stay here for now. We'll both be strangers here, me from Arizona and you from the future. What do you say, Jennifer? Want to make a new home here together?"

He knew he sounded confident, but there was doubt in his voice too. He should have known that with Jennifer, he had no need to be concerned.

She looked up at him, his beautiful woman, and said, "I say yes, Charlie."

EPILOGUE

THE STATUE STOOD IN A small park off the King's Road. Charlie Dawes, focussed on something in the distance, pistol at his side, his coat open to show off the star on his chest.

People came here to sit on the grass at his feet and have lunch, and children ran around him while their parents lazed in the sunshine. No one thought too much about who he was or what he had done, but if they were interested, there was a plaque on its base.

CHARLIE DAWES (AKA DEADEYE DICK)

STAR PERFORMER IN BUFFALO BILL'S WILD WEST SHOW, WHICH PERFORMED DURING THE GOLDEN JUBILEE CELEBRATIONS IN 1887. HE AND HIS WIFE JENNIFER STARTED A COFFEE SHOP NEXT TO THIS PARK.

Below was a further inscription.

THIS STATUE WAS ERECTED BY THE DUCHESS OF BRIDLINGTON AND HER SECOND HUSBAND, BERTIE KENDALL, IN HONOUR OF THEIR GOOD FRIENDS.

Acknowledgements

My thanks go to Noah Chin, who edited this book and offered so many suggestions to make it better, and to Christine Gardner whose help and line editing gave everything an extra polish. Big thanks to Kim Killion for the cover and the whole new sexy look for the Immortal Warriors. Love to my family who are always supportive and understanding, even when I'm writing at Christmas. And lastly but most important of all, thank you to my readers who continue to buy my books.

About the Author

Sara Mackenzie is the author of The Immortal Warriors series. She also writes Historical Romance as Sara Bennett and Evie North.

You'll find all three of them here
https://www.sara-bennett.com/

You can visit her on her Facebook page
https://www.facebook.com/saramackenzieparanormalromance/

While you're there sign up to her Newsletter for the latest news
https://www.facebook.com/saramackenzieparanormalromance/app/152926008054123/

OTHER TITLES BY SARA MACKENZIE